SPECULATIVE HORIZONS

SPECULATIVE
HORIZONS

Edited by Patrick St-Denis

SUBTERRANEAN PRESS 2010

First Edition

ISBN
978-1-59606-336-5

Subterranean Press
PO Box 190106
Burton, MI 48519

www.subterraneanpress.com

This book is dedicated to my mother,
Lorraine Cloutier St-Denis

You battled through breast cancer and
chemotherapy with a grace that never ceased to
amaze everyone around you. I wish I could be
half as good in the face of adversity.

Je t'aime. . .

Table of Contents

Soul Mate by C. S. FRIEDMAN
—9—

The Eve of the Fall of Habesh by TOBIAS S. BUCKELL
—35—

The Stranger by L. E. MODESITT, JR.
—59—

Flint by BRIAN RUCKLEY
—77—

The Death of a Love by HAL DUNCAN
—105—

Soul Mate

C. S. FRIEDMAN

*R*eaders sometimes ask me when I first started writing.
The truth is, I don't really know. I've been telling stories for as far
back as I can remember, and writing them down since the day I first
learned how to hold a pen. The act of writing was compulsive in
my early days, not to be derailed by anything so mundane as school,
chores, or even the need for sleep. I scribbled chapters of a vampire
novel between pages of my biology notes. I doodled starmaps on my
binder covers. And when a fellow student snapped at me "out of my
way, Earthling!" I responded, as any sane teenager would, "who
are you calling an Earthling?"

I'm older now (and a little more discreet about who I discuss
my planet of origin with) but that compulsive element is still part
of my writing. These days it manifests in the form of short story
ideas that just won't go away, no matter how hard I try not to write
them. Oh, I keep telling myself I should be working on my current
novel instead, or some other major life project that really needs to
be taken care of, but they just won't leave me alone. They know

that someday they will get their opening, and then I won't be able to concentrate on anything else until they are safely on paper, ready to be presented to the world at large.

So when Pat invited me to contribute to this anthology, to help him raise money for a worthy cause, I let one of the best ones go free. I hope you enjoy reading it as much as it enjoys being read.

❖

*A*ll things considered, the arts and crafts festival was not as bad as it could have been.

There was a lot of high-end jewelry being sold, polished gold and silver sculpted into interesting shapes, and several booths featured the paintings of prominent abstract artists. The latter was a happy surprise for Josie. A show like this usually had stall after stall filled with representational paintings, passionless renderings of trees and streams and farmhouses and ducks (there always seemed to be ducks), just waiting to be hung on the wall behind an ugly flowered couch. And of course there were always crowds of sunburned tourists standing around each painting, chattering about how wonderful the ruddy hue of that aging barn was, or how that particular beam of sunlight, trickling through the branches of a willow tree, was just the *right* tone of amber. At such times she was acutely aware of the limits of her own vision, and the fact that she could not perceive the same subtle distinctions of color that other people could. Abstract art, by contrast, was a purely private indulgence. It either spoke to you or it didn't. No one else told you what it was supposed to look like, or felt that there was something wrong with you if you could not share their perspective.

She wandered around for nearly an hour before the day's heat finally got to her, then made her way back to the far end of the festival grounds, where her friend Karen had set up her wares. The U-shaped table was located next to a vast, spreading oak tree, whose branches had offered a modicum of shade during the first part of the day. But the afternoon sun had shifted westward, moving the shade away from the display, and the beach umbrella set up to compensate wasn't big enough to shelter the whole table. Racks of crystal earrings seemed to catch on fire as the sunlight hit them, blazing with palpable heat. Did that play up the colors in the glass, or mask them? The only hue that Josie could pick out clearly was a brilliant cobalt at the end of the rack, defiantly cool. But that was hardly a surprise. Most of Karen's more subtle color combinations were lost on her.

"How is business?" Josie asked, settling into a small red plastic chair by the side of the table.

"As you'd expect." Karen reached back into a cooler behind her, pulled out an ice-cold soda, and handed it over. Josie held it against her face for a moment before breaking it open, letting her skin absorb its wonderful chill. "People don't spend as much money in this kind of heat." She sipped from her own soda. "Everything will wind down soon, I expect. The stained glass people have already left. How did your shopping go?"

"There was some nice jewelry. Nothing I desperately need to own. Except for Romero's stuff, which I can't afford." She sighed. "He's got a lotus blossom necklace to die for—art nouveau design, with freshwater pearls in the blossoms—but...well, you know his prices. A real work of art, though."

"You always did liked that art nouveau stuff."

She nodded and took a deep drink from her can, shutting her eyes to savor the cool flow of effervescent liquid down her throat. In the midst of the day's heat, it was almost as good as diving into a waterfall.

"Hey." Karen nudged her with an elbow. "Speaking of works of art."

Opening her eyes once more, Josie followed her friend's gaze across the festival grounds. There was a dirt road dividing their row of tables from the next one, where a row of couch-painting vendors hawked their indistinguishable wares. At the end of the line was a small display of more interesting work, including a few Vernon Miller prints. Bright, bold, and clean of line, they were as refreshing to her as the cool soda had been, and for a moment she forgot her purpose and just admired them. But Karen's elbow in her ribs urged her back to the business at hand, and so she scanned the whole of the stall, wondering what it was that her friend wanted her to look at—

"Oh…"

He stood opposite one of the larger prints, a lithograph that Josie had been admiring earlier in the day. His attention was wholly focused upon the work, as if the rest of the world had ceased to exist. The sense of aesthetic communion was so intense that it seemed almost sexual, and Josie found herself being drawn to both him and the lithograph. Or maybe that had nothing to do with his concentration. Maybe the sight of a man that attractive admiring her favorite artist was a pleasurable thing in its own right. In truth, he was as good to look at as anything she'd seen at the festival. He had dark features and a strong build, and an aura of self-confidence bordering on arrogance which most women found irresistible. His white linen shirt was perfectly pressed, his dark hair perfectly coifed, his leather shoes perfectly polished. He was the kind of man who looked as good as he did because he invested time and effort in doing so. The kind of man you admired in magazines, but did not expect to meet in person.

"Ten bucks says he's gay," Karen whispered.

"You think?"

Karen chuckled. "You know the rule. The pretty ones are always gay, married, or living in their mother's basement."

The stranger turned towards the front of the stall suddenly, as if something on their side of the road had drawn his attention. Josie caught a flash of deep brown eyes as he scanned the fairgrounds, a hint of some exotic heritage in their depths. Not a type she normally dated, but damn, he was good to look at.

"Or a serial killer," she whispered back, completing the formula.

And then, unexpectedly, he looked directly at them, and met Josie's gaze. His eyes fixed on her with the same intensity they had on Miller's artwork, and she could feel herself shiver. Yes, it was a clearly a sexual thing this time. No lithograph to blame it on.

He left the Miller stall behind, and started towards them.

"Holy shit," Karen whispered, and she started straightening out necklaces for cover. Josie lifted up a hand to smooth the stray wisps of her blond hair back into place. It was a hopeless task. A long day of sun and sweat had made her feel like a drowned rat; she couldn't have looked worse for meeting a man like this, she thought, if she'd dressed for the occasion.

And then he was right there in front of her, all tan and gym-toned and looking like he just stepped out of a Bally ad. "I saw you admiring the lithographs."

From somewhere she found her voice. "I like Miller's work a lot."

He smiled. "Then we have that much in common." He glanced down at the table, and reached out to stroke a pair of crystal earrings. He wore no ring, Josie noted, nor was there any tan line to imply that he should be wearing one. Not married, then. *One down.* "Good art speaks to the soul, don't you think?"

"So does bad art." She managed to smile. "It just says things we don't want to hear."

"Perhaps." His smile was winning. His own teeth were perfect. The kind of perfect that didn't come naturally, but had to be paid for, tooth by tooth. "Is all this yours?" He indicated the jewelry.

She shook her head, nodding towards Karen, who offered, "Mine. All hand-made, sterling silver, and the crystal is Swarovski." With a mischievous gleam in her eye she added, "Perhaps there's something here your girlfriend would like?"

A faint smile flickered across his lips as he looked at her; he knew the bait for what it was. "I have no girlfriend."

"A boyfriend, then?" Karen smiled sweetly. "I have body jewelry."

Josie found she was holding her breath. But he only chuckled and turned back to her. "Forgive me," he said, "I'm being rude. Stephan Mayeaux." He offered her his hand.

"Josie Ballard. Josephine, that is. And this is Karen Foster."

He held her hand a moment longer than he had to; the contact made her skin tingle. For a moment—just a moment—it seemed there was a connection between them, something that mere physical touch could not explain. Or was that just wishful thinking on her part? Jesus, she was thinking like the heroine of a cheap romance novel. (Not that she ever read any of those, of course.)

Suddenly the strains of a rippling piano arpeggio dispelled her reverie; it took her a few seconds to recognize the melody as a Bach prelude. He pulled the a cell phone out of his pocket, looked at the caller ID window, and sighed "I'm sorry. Please excuse me. I need to answer this."

He walked down the road a few steps and turned away from them. Josie could sense Karen trying to get her attention, but she didn't make eye contact with her. She was too busy trying not to think about whether or not this man was really flirting with her, and what it might mean if he did.

He's not your type, you know that. Too self-focused. Too meticulous. Probably obsessive/compulsive to boot. How do you make love to a man, if his biggest concern is that his hair might get mussed? He probably lives in the kind of house where nothing is ever out of place. Not a rundown Victorian, stuffed to the rafters with a lifetime of mementos, all in glorious disorder. Like mine. What would he think of that if he saw it?

It was a bad match. Really bad. That much was clear.

Then he snapped his phone shut and turned back to her. "I'm sorry. There's trouble with an incoming shipment. I'm going to have to go back to the gallery and deal with it."

"The gallery?"

"Northpoint Gallery. Out by the lakefront. Mostly I carry things for the tourist trade, but you know...there's a new Miller coming in that I think you might like."

The words came out before she could stop them. "Is that an invitation?"

The dark eyes were fixed on her. Their intensity was unnerving. "If I had your phone number it might be."

Jesus. Jesus. She couldn't date an art dealer. What would happen when he realized that she couldn't see half the things in his world? What would they talk about?

Something small and white nudged her arm. She looked down at the table and saw that Karen was offering a business card to her, blank side up, along with a pen. After a moment's hesitation she took them, and wrote out her number as if in a daze. *Bad idea,* an inner voice cautioned. "Here," she said, giving it to him. Wondering if her smile had ever looked as perfect as his. Maybe she should look into having her teeth whitened.

"I'll call you," he promised. And he nodded a polite farewell to them both before heading back down the road, towards the fairground exit.

The two friends looked at each other. For a moment they both said nothing.

Then Karen sighed. "Just make sure you check out his mother's basement before you sleep with him, will you?

A WOMAN.

He sits in the quiet darkness of his sleek and spotless apartment, moonlight washing over him, and thinks: I have chosen a woman.

He isn't quite sure why it happened. He certainly hadn't planned it. But instinct, as always, was a powerful master. The moment he had felt this one's scrutiny touch him—the moment she had connected to Miller's lithograph, and through that, to him—he had wanted her. Even before he had had seen her face, or learned her name. It was not a desire born of intellect but of instinct, that burning fire deep within his soul which has been banked for far too long. Now the flames are rising up again, and they threaten to consume him whole if he does not feed them the fuel they want.

A woman.

He's known for a some time now that a change is imminent. He is familiar enough with the soul-deep restlessness that precedes such events to know it for what it is, and has already been wondering where it will lead him. Will the next phase of his life be a comfortable and familiar thing, ushered in without effort or hardship? Or does he hunger for something more challenging this time, an experience that will set all his senses alight with fear, so that his new life is birthed in a pool of adrenalin-charged uncertainty? His last few lovers have all been men, so similar in body and mindset that they are all but interchangeable. True, he savors the subtle differences between them as one does a fine wine, reveling in delicate distinctions of taste that only a true connoisseur can detect, while taking perverse pleasure in the fact that no one on the outside can ever share his perceptions. But moving from one to another has been as effortless as crossing the street, a symphony of adaptation. One of them likes silk shirts. Another prefers linen. All movements in the same finely ordered composition.

This…this one will be different. Jazz. Cacophony.

A woman.

He has not taken on challenge like this in a very long time. Several lifetimes, in fact.

Perhaps he is overdue.

Moonlight shivers across the polished floorboards as he picks up his phone, draws out her card, and begins to dial.

JOSIE HAD never been so nervous about a date in her life. Or spent so long preparing for one. It took her hours just to find an outfit to wear—not her usual bohemian garb, flowing with layers of embroidered gauze, but a neater, simpler style, that would hopefully appeal to his meticulous taste—and then hours more to clean up the house to the point where, if he wound up coming inside, he would not get scared away. Not that the place was messy, exactly, but her penchant for hanging onto mementos from all the high points of her life did make for a cluttered house, and he didn't strike her as the kind of man who appreciated clutter as an art form.

This is crazy, she thought. *We probably have nothing in common. Surely he'll figure that out within an hour, and the whole relationship will be over before dessert.*

But then he showed up at her door and all those doubts vanished. Not because she'd necessarily been wrong about him… simply because she didn't care.

He was dressed in a softer mode tonight. Maybe he had sensed that his former appearance was intimidating to her. There were even one or two hairs out of place, as if the wind had disturbed them. Was that a genuine disarray, or simply an artful affectation? She didn't know him well enough to say for sure, but it soothed her nerves to think it might be the former. It made him seem...well, more *human*.

They would find common ground, she told herself. She would make it happen.

But surprisingly little effort was needed in that regard. He took her to a seafood restaurant on the eastern shore of the lake, without even knowing it was one of her favorites. She let him pick out the wine for them, and he chose the same Reisling she would have ordered for herself. He even chose one of her favorite dishes for his own meal, though she'd never said a word about liking it.

It was heartening...but it was also eerie. For a brief moment Karen's warning echoed in her brain, and she wondered if he might not have gained all that knowledge from watching her eat on some former occasion. Would she even know what a stalker looked like, if she met one? But then the conversation turned to other things, things he could not possibly have known about her from simple observation. Passages from literature that had touched her spirit. Musical compositions that made her soul sing with joy, or weep with sorrow. As he shared a glimpse of his own special, secret moments, she was struck by how alike they were, deep inside. As if they were twins who had been separated long ago, now rediscovering each other.

Except for the matter of art.

She didn't have the courage to tell him about her limited vision, or how it affected her perception of the visual arts. Didn't have the heart to explain to him that her familiarity with Jordan

Miller's work had more to do with keeping Karen company on weekends, when she sold her wares at various art festivals, than any greater appreciation of the lithographic medium. That didn't mean that she wasn't a creative soul at heart, but her own preferred medium was the author's pen. Writing was an art form could understand, the subtle gradations of a finely crafted poem as real to her, and as beautiful, as any brush stroke of Da Vinci's was to him.

He will invite me to see his gallery, she thought. With a cold fluttering in the pit of her stomach, at the thought that their strange compatibility, so fragile and new, might not survive the test of such a visit.

But for now, it was enough to eat dessert at an outdoor table overlooking the water, watching the sunset ripple across the waves. Stephan spoke in poetic terms about the color of the light, which was not the most comfortable moment for her, but while he spoke the breeze tousled his hair, and she focused on that. Sometimes she felt as if the man she was with tonight, and the one she had met at the festival, were two different creatures. Or perhaps the first one had become magically transformed, into her perfect suitor.

Really, she thought, she should start writing romance novels herself.

When the meal was over they walked along the beach together, and he kicked off his shoes to feel the wet sand squish between his toes, which was one of her own secret pleasures. They laughed and they talked and maybe they'd had a little too much wine, because they started running down the beach together, splashing through the water like kids. How strange it all was, and how wonderful! As if she had known him all her life. As if they had a thousand memories in common, rather than only a few precious hours.

And in the end she discovered that he did not really mind rumpled clothes, or getting sand in his hair, half as much as she'd expected. Which was a good thing, because neither did she.

"So WHAT do you think?"

The Northpoint Gallery was a sleek, modern construct, whose architecture seemed better suited to uptown Manhattan than a resort town. The darkness of early evening only intensified that effect, glass and steel reflecting back fragmentary images from the more traditional facades surrounding the building, producing a ghostly mosaic that masked what was inside.

It was exactly the kind of place she would have expected him to own, back when she had first met him, but it seemed a strange mismatch to the man she was now dating. She blinked as she entered, trying to reconcile the two identities.

Inside was a gallery as Spartan and sleek as the facade, with stark white walls set at dramatic angles, and strange modern sculptures poised atop pedestals of burnished steel. It resonated money and taste in cold, carefully controlled parameters. The kind of thing she had happily left behind when she'd moved out of the city years ago.

"The yuppies come shopping here when the rustic stuff starts to get to them," he explained. "There are only so many candle shops you can visit before you go mad."

She smiled slightly, trying to feel comfortable in this alien place. "So you cater to their madness."

"It's proven to be a lucrative market. Would you like some coffee?"

Before she could answer, a young Hispanic man emerged from behind one of the angled walls. He was dressed in a silk shirt and expensive designer slacks, and was as meticulously well groomed as Stephan had been back at the fairgrounds. No doubt they shopped at the same boutique, and probably used the same hair gel.

The newcomer raised an eyebrow as he looked at Stephan, then at her, then back to Stephan; the message of incredulity was clear. *You're with a woman?*

"Josephine, this is Pietro, my assistant." He nodded towards him. "Pietro, would you please bring the lady some coffee?"

"Black with sugar," she offered.

Pietro moved off wordlessly to obey. He had the same air that Stephan had once had, the low-key arrogance of an urban sophisticate. But Stephan no longer had that air about him. Could a man change so much in just a few weeks? The thought that she might have inspired such a transformation in him was truly humbling...and also a bit disturbing.

Then he took her around and showed her the artwork. They started with a collection of bronze sculptures, which wasn't half bad. He knew the artist personally, and had interesting stories to tell about each piece. By the time he turned his attention to one of the larger paintings she had a cup of coffee in her hand, that she could play with to mask her nervousness.

But instead of talking about the painting, he just stared at it for a minute, as if something about it was not quite right. "That's odd," he muttered.

"What is?"

He looked back at one of the statues and squinted, as if something about it puzzled him. Then back at the painting. "The light. It's not right." He called out to the back of the store, "Pietro!" When the assistant appeared he asked him, "Have we changed any of our bulbs recently?"

"Not that I'm aware of."

His brow furrowed as he looked back at the painting. "How strange..."

"Light bulbs?" Josie asked.

"Spectrum balanced, to be as close to a neutral white as possible. So that all the colors will read true." He shook his head "Maybe it's an electrical thing. Color temperature drops when the bulbs aren't operating at full capacity. I'll have an electrician check it out in the morning." He turned to her; a warm smile on his lips. "I'll have to bring you back here sometime when you can see everything in the proper light."

The thought that she might be sensitive enough to color that changing a light bulb would matter was almost enough to make her laugh out loud, but she managed to stifle the instinct. "I'd like that," she said solemnly.

"Meanwhile...I have a gift for you."

He took a small, flat box out of his breast pocket and handed it to her. Curious, she opened it. Inside was a vintage gold-and-pearl pendant. Art nouveau.

"Happy two-week anniversary," he told her.

"It's beautiful," she whispered. "I love this style. How did you know?"

He chuckled softly. "We have so much else in common, I took a chance we shared taste in jewelry as well. Here. Let me help you."

He placed the pendant in the hollow of her throat, then reached around to the back of her neck to work the clasp. As he did so she caught sight of Pietro out of the corner of her eye, dark eyes glowering, mouth pursed in obvious disapproval. Perhaps jealousy? Had they been lovers in the past, perhaps? That might explain his expression.

Yes, she thought defiantly, *that's right, Stephan is dating a blond, blue-eyed, nature-loving antique junkie now, who wears peasant shirts and Dr. Scholl sandals. And, by the way, she's a woman. So suck it up, pretty boy!*

IT WAS Karen who suggested a double date. It had been weeks since the two of them had seen each other, she said, and since Josie and her new beau seemed to be inseparable now, it seemed the easiest way to get together.

She sounded faintly bitter about the situation, but that was only to be expected. The two of them had been sisters in all but name for as far back as Josie could remember. This was the first time they'd been apart for so long. And to be fair, Josie really had been neglecting her friends lately. Not by any grand design, of course But there was simply a finite amount of time in the universe, and Stephan Mayeaux was now taking up most of it.

She could not wait for Karen to see how much he had changed. How well they were suited to one another. Surely that chemistry would be evident, even over dinner! Not until now had she realized just how much she wanted her best friend to approve of this man. Not until that happened could her relationship be truly perfect.

Karen suggested they meet at an Italian restaurant, a quiet and friendly place where they could all chat comfortably. Her own date was a shy sort who didn't add much to the conversation, but Stephan was nothing short of charming. His business with the gallery had given him enough experience with art shows that he was soon sharing anecdotes with Karen as if they were old friends, and Josie was flushed with happiness. When Karen excused herself from the table after the main course she did the same, anxious for a moment alone with her to hear what she thought.

Karen said nothing to her on the way to the ladies' room. When as she entered, she walked down past the row of stalls, checking to see if they were occupied.

"Well?" Josie asked impatiently. "What do you think?

After confirming that all the stalls were empty, Karen hesitated "I think there's something not right about him, Josie. I'm sorry."

Josie was stunned. "I don't understand"

"Do you not see what he's doing? Or do you just not care?"

A cold shiver ran down Josie's spine. "See what?"

"That he's copying your mannerisms. Your expressions. Even the cadence of his voice is becoming like yours." She shook her head. "I met him when you did, Josie. Remember? I know what he was like, before he started dating you. And I tell you, he's copying your body language now. Maybe just unconsciously, I don't know. But that's still pretty weird, don't you think?"

Josie blinked. The accusation was…well, it was so bizarre she could barely absorb it. Finally she managed to force out, "I'm sure you're imagining this."

"You've got this little thing you do with your spoon when you get soup, do you know that? You run it around the rim of the bowl just before you start eating. Just a little unconscious thing, I'm sure; I've watched you do it for years. And tonight…he did it too. That's very strange, Josie." Her eyes narrowed. "No. It's more than strange. It's downright creepy."

"You think he's mocking me?"

"No. No. I don't think it's that at all. It's just that…how much do you know about him? I mean *really* know about him?"

"I know that we have great chemistry," she said defiantly. "And couples with great chemistry sometimes come to resemble one another. Sometimes they even have mannerisms in common, just like you're describing."

"Yes—after ten years of marriage, not three weeks of dating."
She paused "You know, I hate to bring this up, but there's a kind
of mental illness where a man will adopt the personality of other
people. Maybe he's got something like that."

"You watch too much TV," she snapped.

"That doesn't mean I'm wrong," she snapped back.

Josie turned away; she did not want her friend to see the tears
that were coming to her eyes. After a moment Karen reached
out and put a hand on her shoulder; the contact was comforting.
"Josie, I love you. You know that. I wouldn't do anything to hurt
you, ever. But this guy...something about him is just not right.
You've got to trust me on this one."

"You think I should break up with him?"

The hand fell away. She heard Karen sigh. "I think that's your
choice to make. But I would, if I were you. In a heartbeat."

Josie did not answer her. After a moment of silence, she heard
Karen walk away. The door of a booth squeaked open, then closed,
and she heard the snick of a lock.

She left the rest room.

There was a short hallway right outside the door. She leaned
against the wall there, her shoulders trembling, and tried to pull
herself together. She couldn't let Stephan see her like this. He
wouldn't understand.

Karen's hurt, she thought, *and she's jealous. We've been inseparable for nearly five years now, and suddenly someone has come between
us. Of course she's going to see the worst in him. Of course she's going
to hope that I'll end it.*

It wasn't a perfect explanation, she knew. It probably wouldn't
stand up to close inspection in the clear light of morning. But it
was something she could cling to right now, to get her through the
rest of the meal without tears, and that was what mattered most.

"You okay?" Stephan asked her.

She huddled down into the passenger seat of his car, resting her cheek against the sleek black Italian leather. "I'm okay," she said quietly.

"You were pretty quiet after you came back to the table."

"I had a lot to think about."

He was driving with one hand through the steering wheel, his wrist resting on the central column. It was a position that would block the airbag if there were an accident. Josie's mother was always on her case about her doing that.

I love you, she thought miserably. *I don't want there to be anything wrong with you.*

"Something your friend Karen said?"

All the rest of the meal, she had watched him closely. Listened to him closely. Trying to decide if Karen was right. Wanting, with all her heart, to believe she was wrong.

"She thought we were moving too fast," she said. It was better to give him some kind of explanation than try to deny that anything had happened. "She just wanted me to be careful, that's all."

"Careful?" There was an edge to his voice now; he clearly didn't like the fact that Karen was interfering in their relationship. "Careful about what?"

She shrugged

He looked over at her. "If there's a problem, we can talk about it. You know that. There's nothing we can't handle, if we do it together."

A lump rose in her throat. "I know," she whispered.

He looked back at the road. They were approaching a major intersection, where the light had changed while they were talking.

He didn't stop.

Cars screeched to a halt as they skidded out of the way, trying to avoid a collision. Stephan turned his wheel wildly, trying to avoid a truck that was suddenly in his path. Time seemed to slow down as Josie grabbed the edges of her seat, her heart pounding so hard she thought it would burst from her chest. Everything seemed to be in slow motion. Cars screeched past her window at a surreal pace, giving her time to work out just how badly she would be crushed if they did not turn aside in time.

And then, as quickly as it had begun, it was over. Stephan managed to pull over to the curb without hitting anyone, while the other cars began to sort themselves out and move past him. No one had been hurt, thank God, but Josie was badly shaken. So was Stephan, apparently; his hands were gripping the wheel so tightly that his knuckles were white.

For a moment they both just stared out the window, unable to speak. Then he reached down and put the car in park, and turned to face her. The look in his eyes was terrible, but it was not fear she saw there. It was rage.

"*You are colorblind,*" he accused.

Her mouth hung open in astonishment. She didn't know how to respond.

"You should have told me!"

"What the hell business is it of yours?" She was angry herself now, that he would follow up such a nerve-wracking experience with this crazy scene. Here she was, still shaking after a near brush with death, and he was yelling at her about some piddling handicap that she hadn't confessed to him? "What difference does it make, anyway? It's my problem, not yours."

For a moment she thought that he was going to hit her. He looked that angry. Then, with a muttered curse, he fumbled his seat belt open, thrust his door open, and exited the car. When he was clear of the door he slammed it shut behind him, so hard that the whole vehicle shook.

She sat there in shock for a moment, then climbed out of the car herself. He was already halfway down the block, and walking away at a swift clip.

"Stephan!"

He turned to look back at her. His expression was so terrible that it made her take a step backwards. Rage. Pure rage.

At her? Over what?

Then he turned his back to her again and continued down the street. And it was all she could do to sink back down into the passenger seat, shaking, and try to catch her breath.

What the hell was that about?

GALLERY VANDALIZED

Northpoint Gallery was vandalized last night, some time between 10 and 11 P.M. Locals heard crashing noises coming from inside the building and called in an alarm, but by the time police arrived, over $100,000 worth of original artwork had been destroyed, with extensive damage to the interior of the building.

Sheriff Leon Marshall is heading Northpoint's investigation into the case. While few details are being released at this time, the nature of the damage has prompted speculation that the vandalism may have been an act of rage, possibly directed at the owner of the gallery, Mr. Stephan Mayeaux.

Mr. Mayeaux has thus far declined to comment upon the matter.

"KAREN. ARE you there? Please pick up if you are."

Silence.

"Karen, please call me as soon as you get in. Please. I need to talk to you."

Silence on the line. Faint static in the distance. It continued on like that for a few more seconds, then the dial tone finally kicked in.

No one was going to answer.

Her heart cold with misgiving, Josie finally hung up. God alone knew what Karen would think when she got home and checked her recorder. Josie had left at least half a dozen messages to date, and that was not counting all the times she had called and said nothing. But surely it wasn't unreasonable for her to be concerned. Karen was the kind of person who was joined at the hip to her cell phone, and the only way she'd be out of touch for this long was if sunspots had wiped out all reception on earth.

So something was wrong.

Josie paced back and forth across the kitchen, trying to burn off some of her nervous energy. Stephan hadn't talked to her since that night in the car. And now there was the news that his gallery had been vandalized, and all his precious artwork destroyed, within an hour of their fight. Every time she tried to figure out what could possibly have happened, she got a cold knot in the pit of her stomach. Karen could have helped her sort it all out. But Karen was missing. Her whole world was upside down.

She hadn't called Stephan yet. She kept picking up the phone to do so, and once she even dialed his number, but she always hung up before the connection could be made. She didn't know what to say to him. She needed for him to call her first, to tell her that everything was all right. Or at least to say something that would allow her to believe that he hadn't destroyed his gallery himself.

What the hell had happened in the car?

No matter how many times she went over the incident in her mind, it just made no sense to her. They'd been driving along, had a near-accident, and suddenly he had gotten angry at her for being colorblind. No; suddenly he had *realized* she was colorblind. That was the really weird part of it. The more she went over the scene in her mind, the more she became convinced that she was watching his actual moment of revelation. The knowledge had come to him in the wake of the accident, seemingly out of nowhere, and then he had turned on her.

It just made no sense.

She ached for him, as she had never ached for anyone before. Having him missing from her life was like having part of her soul excised; a spiritual amputation. But what would she say to him, if she did call? Even if she were desperate enough to beg for forgiveness, or grovel to bring him back…what exactly would she be groveling about?

With a sigh she got up and began to change the coffee filter, preparing to make another pot. She'd switched to decaf hours ago; her nerves couldn't handle anything stronger. Her left pinky finger was twitching, which is something it did when she was stressed to the breaking point. A warning sign.

And then the doorbell rang.

For a moment she froze. Then, hands shaking, she put the filter down on the counter, oblivious to the brown liquid that was leaking out of it.

She hurried to the front hallway, drew in a deep breath, and opened the door.

It was Stephan.

He said nothing to her. Just waited. After a moment she backed away to give him room to come in. His anger seemed to have subsided, but there was a strange look in his eyes, that warned her to keep her distance. Was it possible he was dangerous? She didn't want to believe he would hurt her, but after that scene in the car, anything was possible.

There is something not right about him, Karen had warned her.

But he only walked quietly into the living room, and she followed, equally silent. For a moment he just stood there, as if gathering his thoughts, and she waited.

"I'm sorry," he said at last.

The knot in her gut loosened a tiny bit. She felt tears coming to her eyes, and struggled to fight them back.

"I'm sorry things are moving so fast," he continued. "Usually the process is much more...leisurely."

The dark brown eyes met hers. She could see herself in them, like reflections in tiny mirrors.

"Your life and mine are incompatible," he told her. "I can't handle both of them at once. And I can't go back. I've tried that before, and it just doesn't work."

He put his hands on the sides of her face, cupping her cheeks gently. She felt herself trembling.

Leaning over, he kissed her softly on the forehead. "I'm sorry," he whispered.

His left pinky twitched against her cheek.

A sudden wave of panic came over her. She tried to pull away from him, but it was hard to move. Hard to do anything other than surrender to his touch. It felt as if they were attached, somehow, and she could not separate from him without tearing her flesh to pieces.

"What are you?" she whispered. She struggled to calculate the distance she'd have to go to get to the front door, the alarm pad, the knife rack in the kitchen...all too far, too far away. "What do you want?"

He didn't answer. His eyes were dark and cold, without a hint of kindness in them.

And then she finally managed to pull away from him, and tried to run. But her feet felt like hundred-pound weights were attached to them, and she only managed two steps before she stumbled and fell. He knelt by her side and took her face in his hands again, and she could not break free of his grasp.

And then she looked up at him, and saw what he had become.

And screamed.

"It should have been gentler," her lover said quietly. "I would have taken you in your sleep. Nestled you in my arms. A peaceful transition. That's how it usually goes."

Visions began to race through Josie's mind. Memories from her youth. From young adulthood. From yesterday. In the wake of each one there was a spark of pain, and then the memory was gone. Completely gone. As though it had never existed in the first place.

"You should have told me you were imperfect," the creature that had been Stephan admonished her. "I never would have chosen you, if I'd known"

The memory of Karen flickered through her mind, and then vanished. Her last memory. Tears ran down her face, but she no longer remembered why she was crying.

The last thing she saw, before darkness claimed her, was her own face gazing down at her.

PEACE.

The life he has lived for so long is gone, and with it all the hungers and passions and insecurities that once attended it. He can no longer see color properly—that is the unfortunate cost of this transition—but now that he has changed, he no longer has the same driving need to see color. That was a feature of Stephan, and Stephan is dead now. Josie takes pleasure in language, and now, finally, he has the capacity to understand that gift. How beautiful a simple phrase can be, when perfectly crafted! How thrilling, the discovery of a new and expressive word!

Memories flood his brain, reshaping neural pathways in their wake. Her parent's love. Her first kiss. Her final moment of fear. All his now.

No...all hers.

Rising up from beside the body on the floor, Josie Ballard looks around for matches. When she finds them on the fireplace mantle, she sets fire to furnishings in the living room, then calmly walks out of the front door, trusting that the flames will not be seen by neighbors until she has cleared the neighborhood. After that, it does not matter if the whole house burns or not, so long as the death within that house has enough of an explanation to satisfy the police.

There was a time that she would have worried about someone identifying the body, and seeking out the truth of what had happened to it...but experience has taught her, down through the years, that such a thing is not possible. The flesh she is leaving behind does not have an identity that anyone will be able to put a name to, no matter what techniques they apply.

It occurs to her that she should write a poem about this whole experience. As she heads off into the night, she begins to works out what its meter will be.

The Eve of the Fall of Habesh

TOBIAS S. BUCKELL

everal years ago I came across a dramatic image of a hut on stilts on a beach. It inspired a story where I created a magic system that eats life when used. After that story I had a striking image in my head of a city filled with tiny, wizened and aged children begging on sidewalks, victims of magic overuse. This story was my way of putting that image into words.

❖

abesh, you beautiful stinking whore of a city.

I love you so.

The sun is grim this morning from the street. There's a haze in the air giving the glowing ball its grit and waver. My brother says the Sea People are burning the Kopach just five miles north. Which means the haze comes from the cinders of huts, crops, and burned flesh.

Thus do we inhale and exhale the destruction of our cousins outside the city walls.

But Habesh goes on, as always.

I glance upward, up the thick stone towers of Pophis where I'm headquartered. Cheap to live in, as most people near Market remain convinced that the towers, once part of the original city walls and its watchtowers, would fall at any moment due to their age.

But I know they are as solid as the foundations of Habesh itself, sunk into the granite of the cliffs of Elkatoa.

This city is going nowhere.

The towers will stand.

At least, I think, until the Sea People burst through like water through a dam.

And even then, the city will abide.

But this morning won't. Not with this dallying.

I sweep my long cloak around me and check the small piece of paper a runner delivered me last night.

The consignorii have a target for me.

MY TARGET begs in an arterial street feeding into the heart of Habesh: the Market. The leaders of the city have marked him.

And here I am.

But first, the Market.

It's not a square, like in many cities. It's a great oval plaza. And even the oval isn't so much dedicated to the Market. The Market is flexible. There are some pit houses, dedicated to the city patrons, scattered throughout. The House of Defensive Arguments, marble columns rising high, crowned with the fires of Justice blazing at their tops, sits on the northwest loop.

Other civic institutions stand against the flood of the Market, but the consignorii relocated most of those to Ruling Hill.

So the Hall of the Gods no longer hosts the ancient objects of worship, but now the tall building is host to half a mile of stalls. Shouting merchants, screeching birds, bartar, and the smoke of thousands of animals and roots and cooking fires replace the brazen fires and sacrifices of supplicants. There are warehouses and common grounds and temporary tent cities and minstrels and plays and priests of every belief shouting their truths in exchange for alms.

That is the joy of Habesh. A single-minded dedication to the selling of everything you can ever imagine.

Out on the rim of the oval the ferocity of the commerce of thousands and thousands fades. But the traffic of incoming and outgoing via cobblestone is like a river, the trickling sound of feet over stone replacing a brook's babble.

Vendors sell meat on a stick or in a pie alongside the roads, and beggars lie along the gutters.

I'm looking for a particular beggar.

"Hello Bruse," I say, coming up behind him. "I'm invested to take back the powers granted to you by the All, as taught and allowed to you via the Defensive Council of Habesh. This is due the use of them in a cowardly, criminal, and consistently rogue-like manner, as confirmed by the Princips of the House of Defensive Arguments."

Bruse's head barely reaches my chest. He turns to look at me with oversized, rheumy eyes even wider with startlement.

His skin is wrinkled and loose, pale from spending too much time in the shadows, and his hair is patchy. But he moves swiftly against me. A faint blue aura twinkles in the air around him, and then a blast of air strikes me true in the stomach.

It is strong enough to throw me back several feet into a wooden cart, and I bounce off the oversized iron-rimmed wheels with a grunt.

All I can see of my quarry is a foot disappearing around the corner.

What looks like an old lady helps me to my feet. "Hello contragnartii, what a blow you took," she croaks.

I instinctively grab my belt and the tiny purse wrapped to it, catching her withered little hand. I twist it, and she half sobs out a scream.

With a sigh I squatted before her. "How old are you?" I ask gently.

A grubby, nervous face regards me. She hasn't washed in days, and I can see bruises from where other beggars have hit her to chase her away from the prime spots. Like this street corner. "I'm nine, contragnartii."

It is young. They seem to be getting younger all the time, the progeric refuse spit out of the spellyards and magic workhouses.

I finger out several coins into the palm of my hand where ancient-seeming nearby eyes won't spot them, and with a touch almost as deft as the most skilled pickpocket in Habesh, pass them into her hands. "Make it last," I whisper, and take off in pursuit of Bruse.

ANY CONTRAGNARTII worth his salt or silver has a network of informers, spies and grifters. I know where Bruse is headed: the soup tents.

Our greatest villains are often our daily habits.

Bruse's arch-enemy is the comfort of potato and leeks swimming in a salty broth and a cup of wine in a soup tent along Dinner Row. I walk along the backs of the tens, in the gutter, my boots slushing through excrement and piss and garbage.

He thinks it's safe because it is in public, packed among hungry people, and even if the exits are closed off he can rip a hole through the thick canvas of the tall tent with a knife to make his escape.

He thinks, no doubt, to himself, that an altercation would bring the Street Guards.

But this is all good defense against the street. No one in the tents gives a damn about what a contragnartii is up to. The official cape and the seal of the city on the clasp under one's throat meant they'd leave me the hell alone.

And not just because I work for the city, but because I can summon up a spell that rips the ability to do any magics right out of their skulls.

That's why Bruse is running. The ability to throw airblasts in the dog-eat-dog world among Habesh's fallen is a useful talent. And Bruse doesn't want to lose it.

But he's attacked someone important, or been accused once too often of using magic for ill gains.

Which leads to me, carefully slicing the back of the tent open, peeking through the slit, and ducking inside.

I stand right behind Bruse once again.

Wooden benches wobble their way down the old brick street, now the inside of the permanent soup tent. People fill the darkened areas between the poles with their flickering torches, moving around, conversation bubbling. Most of them sit at the tables, slurping soup and watered down wine. There is a kitchen nearby, made of mortar and stone, with a chimney at the top that pokes up through the tent fabric and is stained by the leaks from around that joint.

The air is moist and warm.

This time I don't have to Announce to Bruse. I raise my hands, reaching deep down inside myself, and let slip a tiny bit of my lifeforce as the air around my hands and forearms twinkle.

There is a small sense of loss. I have sacrificed a small measure of my life's essence to fuel this piece of magic. Is it five minutes of my life? Or an hour?

When my fingers touch the back of Bruse's neck, he gasps and twists away, but I can see by the horror in his eyes he knows the reaction is too late.

"You pig's dick!" he screams, raising his hands, then realizes there is nothing he can do.

"You knew this was going to happen," I retort. "Why run and make a scene? Now everyone knows you've been stripped of your talent."

He's breathing heavily, something running through his head. And then he pulls his knife out and leaps for me.

This is not unexpected. Loss, grief, they take many expressions among peoples. Ennui, tears, rage...action.

The tent is crowded: slipping away from the rusty point of his knife means shoving a burly man away from me as I draw a pair of short swords.

I parry Bruse's first and second thrusts easily. He's depended on his magical blasts of air for all his fighting life. He may have once served on the city walls, as most do who are taught a fighting magic, but only ever learned the basics of fighting with a blade.

It isn't hard to hit him with the flat of one of my blades and move in to disarm him.

"No! Let him live!" Two young boys and a girl break out of the door of the kitchen. The youngest raises his hands and strikes me with a mild bolt of fire that hits the tip of my swords.

I drop them both before the heat can burn my palms.

"Stop there," I shout, holding my hands up. "I do not have to touch you to strip you of your magics, I can do it as long as I can see you."

"We know, but you're naturally old," the girl says. She has oak-brown eyes and skin and silky black hair. "You conserve yourself: I'll bet it *costs* to do what you do, the further away you are from your prey. Just like it would cost more for Aylei here to burn you alive, rather than just startle you."

She's right. "I wasn't going to kill him," I say. "Just disarm him and stop him from killing me. You are willing to interfere with the city's business?"

That gets me a haughty look. "The city is dying. The Sea People will be at the walls soon enough. Habesh has other things to worry about than Bruse. Leave him to us. Please."

I think about defending my honor for just a moment, then laugh. My job is done, I have no desire to spend on magic. "What do you want with Bruse?"

"We're leaving Habesh," the girl says. "And Bruse is helping us."

"He'll cut your throats for your money the moment your back is turned to him," I tell her.

Surprisingly, to both Bruse and me, she nods. "We know, and we have anticipated that. But now, more than ever, I doubt it. He needs us almost as much as we need him."

"Well then, don't let me stop you," I say.

The girl looks just behind me. "Okay Liat, let's go. We got what we came for."

I twist around, a cold rivulet of fear in my gut. The space behind me shimmers blue, and out of the air forms another little girl with blue eyes and ratty hair.

Liat walks past me, tapping the sharpened dagger in her hand against her forehead in a mock salute. "G'day, contragnartii."

Everyone stares at the group of children. It's not something you see anymore in Habesh. Most of the children are drafted to serve on the city walls, or had been sent to defend the

Kopach. The rest work the Spellyards and factories. Or had fled the city the day the Great Sea Fleet arrived on the horizon of the Roranraka Sea.

I pick up my short swords and leave through the back of the tent, annoyed by thinking about the impending war. But it's in the air, literally. The black pall of the burning Kopach is always an upward glance away.

The Sea Peoples, scattered across their archipelagos and island chains all throughout the Roranraka, are subject to the whims of storm and tide that brew in the Roranraka. They'd never attacked the Elkatoan coast before. Usually they trade exotic foods, spices, and rare metals along Elkatoan harbors in order to get access to the forests.

That is how things worked, until two years ago, when the meta-consignorii of the four greatest Elkatoan cities plotted together to deny them access to the dwindling lowland forests. The cities wanted to guarantee the survival of what forest was left. The meta-consignorii thought the varied islands and traders weak and non-militaristic.

Everyone thought this, until several hundred ships appeared on the horizon. Each ship represented an island, or a tribe, of the Sea Peoples. They brimmed with warriors. Trade failed: now they take the land they need by force.

They need the wood to build their stilt villages to protect against the daily floods of the Roranraka. They need it to build their massive ocean-crossing, island-connecting ships.

But who could have known there are so many Sea Peoples, and that the Roranraka is so much larger than any person suspected, containing in its vastness all these Sea Peoples?

Ignorance is the death of many, I guess. And that includes cities and countries as equally as men.

At the edge of Dinner Row I stop at a wooden pavilion with lace curtains and rain drapes.

Only the most powerful and rich eat here. Though judging by the empty tables, most of them have left the city, fleeing for the mountains.

I walk to the back, where the cook is stacking his pots in crates. "I want a meal," I demand.

"We are done. There is no one left. The Sea People are here. Go to the soup tents."

I know I'm taking my anger at being beaten by the kids and having to chase Bruse out on this man, but it does not change my response. "Look at who I am, cook. The rich are addicted to your beautiful little meats and your sauces. Maybe it's because you slip a little spell over each meal. I'm not sure, but I'm willing to try stripping whatever it is you have from you if you don't give me a damn meal, you traitor to the city."

He looks startled, but understands. "Fine, why not. I'm leaving the food anyway, I can only take the tools of my trade. The city is dead."

My eyes narrow. "You shouldn't talk like that."

"And you're scared. At least I have a talent I can use anywhere. What you do, it is only for the city's leaders. And soon, they'll be dead. You can't flee, there is nothing else for you."

"Do you know who you're talking to?" I hiss.

"Of course, contragnartii. You can strip me of my magic, and it would make no effect on my ability to cook great meals." He waves his hand around the kitchen. "But still, take whatever you want, anyway, threats aside."

My mouth waters: there are racks of lamb and other delicious meats and still steaming breads.

I'd bring my brother home a feast he would never forget.

But heavy boots tramping the wooden floorboards get my attention. Five City Guard in full armor and helmets walk up to me. One of them is holding his hands out in front of him: he's a Locator.

"Contragnartii Jazim?" the Locator asks.

"I am Jazim, yes."

"Come with us."

The Guard clusters around me as they march me away from the rich smells of the kitchen.

THERE IS a whiff of ominousness to Ruling Hill, I've always felt. Even as contragnartii, walking into the crooked alleys of government edifices and climbing the stone stairs toward the center of power in the city, I always feel...nervous.

That Ruling Hill is built on the charred remains of the previous rulers' final stand, its flagstones the walls of their fortress, is an irony that is today not far from my mind.

An irony I need to banish quickly from my thoughts as I approach the large moat that leads to the stone behemoth where the consignorii dwell.

The spiked gates swing aside with a soulful shriek, and grim mercenary soldiers, not Guardsmen, wait behind them.

A short and wizened inquisitor stands by the atrium. He grasps my forehead with ashy hands, green eyes looking deep into mine, and declares me loyal to the consignorii.

Once he does that, Yamis and two consignorii I am unfamiliar with stride out to face me.

"Your Allness," I say politely, and bow, then kiss the extended thumbtip.

"Tell us about the children," Yamis says, his voice sizzling like rain on outdoor cookfire.

I recount what happened, talking up my skill at tracking down Bruse, but Yamis could care less. "The children!" He shouts. "Have they left yet?"

"I don't know," I reply honestly.

Yamis sighs and grabs my forehead. He is another inquisitor, but like anyone important, only uses his taught skill sparingly, less he hasten himself toward his own end, like Bruse.

But now Yamis is digging his way through my head. I can feel it, a ripple across my thoughts. Memories of the day are springing back to me, then stopping, jumping around, and stopping again until Yamis had seen everything he wanted.

His fingers twinkled blue as he let go of my head. "It is true," he told the other two. "It is them."

I'm not sure what is going on here, but I realize they don't care a bit about Bruse: they're focused on the children.

It makes a sudden sort of sense. All the children not already drafted to defend the city have fled, either taken by their families or friends, or escaped by their own means.

These children are late to the game. An oddity. The consignorii want to press them into service, or get them into a weapons factory.

Yamis must have some faint touch with my mind still, as he shakes his head. "You're only partially correct," he growls. "They're all escapees from the factories. Maybe a hundred. They've been sharing skills back and forth, *teaching* each other magics."

I try to hold in my shock. Magic is a gift from the All, the chance to tap into the raw power of life. Lest it consume us any further than it already did, the Nariaad specifies that no one should learn more than a single spell.

To do otherwise is to claim yourself a god.

The Songs of Demiurgiastes tell of the Novidei who dared to become gods, back when the world was a whole land. Men who learned all, then died as it consumed them like a fire from within. Their battles against the All, and the gods who protected it, cleaved the land, and water poured from under the earth rivers and filled the chasms, giving us the oceans. These were things everyone knew from near-birth.

Here in Habesh, one of the duties of the consignorii is to listen and watch for teaching, a sin graver than any other.

These children lived once in the same Spellyard, but came from the high foothills of the mountains, the peninsular areas, and all up and down the coast of Elkatoa, as well as the gutters of Habesh. And somehow, despite the close eye of their guards and the brutal atmosphere of the yards, they had collaborated in snatched moments and taught each other.

To escape, they'd killed guards, and magically dug tunnels under the Spellyards. They'd created shields to stop pursuers, and cast mental confusion to slip away into the streets.

An entire dormitory of children has been lost to the city, the consignorii explains to me.

"We will hunt them down and hang them," I promise, knowing this was what is expected of me. It still tastes sour, though. Only the consignorii teach magic, and the one skill you are granted, if it is needed, is the only skill you'll ever be granted. Who would risk ending the world, ending magic, and all else, by teaching another their own skills? The Nariaad made clear the consequences, through stories of the beginning of the Roranraka Sea and the history of the lands.

Yamis shakes his head. "It sounds heretical for me to say this," he sighs. "But we need them back in the factories to help defend the walls. Habesh must stand. After we repel the Sea Peoples, then we will hang them all."

It does rank of heresy.

But then, for Habesh, it is a dark time.

"Go find the children," Yamis orders me. "And bring them back to us that we may bind them to the factories. And this time, they will not break their shackles."

There is dark certainty in his voice.

I'm hoping he doesn't look into my thoughts right now. I'm scared of what heresy they're proposing, and what it means for the survival of the city. Surely the All will not tolerate a violation of this sort.

It is right there, in the atrium with the consignorii, that I realize Habesh is doomed for sure.

And I am doomed with it.

JUST IN the hour since I've left the streets something has changed. There is a sense of panic. Any moment the last chances to escape will be shut off, with the roads out of the city dominated by the Sea Peoples.

Habesh will fight for its life like a cornered animal.

But for those who are not willing to stand behind it, they must leave now.

Furtive groups move quickly through the streets toward the distant walls with packs strapped to their backs. They do not meet the eyes of anyone else walking the street. They are like awkward grey ghosts, sidling along the alleys, trying not to be noticed.

For it's a certain kind of treason. Not that the Guard has time to deal with them and their cowardice. The walls are shut, but that doesn't mean there weren't small portices, designed to let scouts and smugglers out.

A high fee is all it takes to get someone with access to these area of the wall to let you out. And then you just have a fast jog to skirt the advancing armies.

And the children are mixed into one of these nervous crowds.

It will be a tough exercise to ferret them out.

Just to hand them over to be used as magical automatons.

Yes, there is some strong seed of doubt in my mind. And it troubles me to look into my soul and find someone different staring right back.

I have to shake it away, move over the cobblestones faster than the dispirited cowards around me, and make my way to one of the sharks poaching on them.

His name is Kish. A terrier of a man, who looks like he should be digging around the inside of a small hole hunting rats. I find him in one of his many haunts, and he stands up to run when he sees me, but I shake my head. "I need your help."

"Your help usually costs me more than I make," Kish complains. Rightfully.

"You don't make a profit," I tell him. "You help me, and then you get to keep your powers of persuasion. If you do not help me, I decide you are using them in a matter that does not honor the All and the City."

I've never put it quite so bluntly. Kish licks his lips and moves from one foot to another, like a nervous messenger.

I glance over at the small cart next to him. "You're leaving, I see."

"Leading one more group out under the Trumpet Gate," Kish says. "I'd offer you a place, but your brother..."

"Let's get back to why I'm here," I snap, cutting that piece of conversation down. "There's a street tough, Bruse, used to run up and down the edge of the market. Know whom I'm talking about?"

Kish does. He has a mind for those things.

"If he's leaving the city, where would *he* do it?"

"Well..." Kish looks thoughtfully up the pall of dark smoke over the city, and then quickly looks back down at his feet. "The old King's Road, by the Spellyards."

In a flash, I understand why the children chose Bruse. Who would think that they'd use an escape route near the very place they'd probably escaped?

THE SPELLYARDS are heavily guarded and gated, the compounds filled with squat, square buildings with massive granite plinths that would look like civic, or religious buildings, if not for their featurelessness. No paint, no carvings, no nothing.

Tough, brutish Guardsmen in full armor stand on the tops of the Spellyard walls, looking out over the courtyards and buildings, ready to stop escapees.

Through a set of gates, in the distance, I can see tiny bodies trudging from one building to another.

Whether it is swords of fire, or magical shields, each of them gives up a piece of their life, their connection to the All, to create these things.

Wasted potential and failed spells waft continuously out of the massive chimneys, the blue sparkle of life disippating over the city as the winds take it for themselves.

The sight weighs heavy on me.

"*That's* why you're congragnaritii," says a voice from by my elbow. "I see."

I jump, whipping around toward the blur in the air, and pull one of my short swords.

The ratty-haired Liat drops her invisibility and holds her hands up in the air. "Truce," she says, rope bracelets sliding back from her wrists to expose manacle marks burned into her skin. I stare at them for a long moment.

"You read minds and hide from sight," I say, still startled, wondering if I was about to be ambushed. Then I realize I am standing right in front of a Spellyard gate. Liat is the one in danger. My confidence returns, and with it, a righteous anger. "You sin against the All."

Liat looks over at the Spellyard and holds up her burned hands. She begins to walk away, and I follow her. Let her talk, let her lead me closer to her friends. "My brother used to sing me the Songs of the Demiurgiastes and the Naiad: it said there we were given our talents freely as gifts from the All, and should gift others with their benefits in the same way. My family were hillfolk shepherds, we came to the city during a drought. We knew no one in the city, so when my family died, I was taken and forced to use my talents to create things for the city. That is no gift. And it troubles you as well, watching your brother slowly die, all his life used up, living in that little dark tower you call home…"

"Stay out of my mind," I hiss, my voice breaking. "Please." I should rip her abilities from her right now. I can feel the tingle in my hands as I get ready.

But there's a commotion in front of us. It's Bruse. He's getting the life kicked out of him by four over-muscled thugs.

He has no way to defend himself, other than to curl up into a ball of rags, his wrinkled hands over his face.

"It's Bruse," Liat says, and runs toward him.

This is not my problem.

This child has seen the inside of a Spellyard, a tougher place than any street.

I watch her slam into the nearest man, and he backhands her with a casual fury that leaves her folded in half on the dirty cobblestones, a tiny thread of blood trickling down her nose.

The smart thing to do is walk away.

But is it? The consignorii will rip into my mind, just like the child did. Then I will be shackled and working on the inside of a Spellyard.

I'm doomed. Whether it is the Sea People or the consignorii.

One of the men is standing over Bruse, ready to kick his skull in as I walk up to them, my fingers crackling. "Leave," I say, my voice strident and calm and full of authority, as if I have the skill of convincing.

The four of them look at me, and pause.

"*Now.*"

The city is on the edge of chaos, but they don't want to lose their connection to the All, whatever skill it is they each possess. They grudgingly step back.

And I am left with the fruits of my treachery and heresy: A child and a broken thief.

WHY DO it?

I think about that as I walk along the street, my boots echoing off the facades of taverns and cramped buildings around us. Bruse is slung over my shoulder as he weighs next to nothing—no more than some feathery skeleton. Liat limps along by my side, still dazed.

We're passing into the Tannery district where the smell of curing leather is strong enough to make you gag.

But here, on this particular road, it begins to fade.

Stunning goddesses of women stand in open windows, on balconies, and by the doors to winehouses. Their hair is long and trussed in perfect knots, their bosoms massive and pert, their long legs slip out of carefully cut dresses. The air smells sweet, of flowers and incenses and things I can't identify that make my head swim. I find myself missing steps as I walk by and women coo at the three of us.

Liat's eyes are wide.

We stop in front of a shop advertising quality hides, where I barely recognize the two figures before me, until they realize who I am.

And suddenly the magic is gone, fading away into a faint turquoise in the dark tavern. The two grandmotherly women in front of me curse. "Jazim, we paid you already!"

I wave her cautious indignation away. "Yelena, Doria, this child and man need somewhere to rest, they were attacked."

"So you come here? What are you going to do, sell the child to the Spellyards?"

They have no reason to trust me. I am not the helping type. They're suspicious. "Do it or the next time you walk out the door looking to get someone in here to sample your 'hides' they'll only see overdried leather," I snap.

It has the effect I want. They'd stab me in the back, if they dared. But the city's oldest trade relies on convincing the clients through illusion. The illusion that these women are flawless creatures.

And I can rip that ability away from them in the blink of an eye.

So Liat and Bruse get a room in the back. It is a quiet place, with thick walls and luxurious drapes. It is clearly normally a refuge for Yelena, Doria, and the others.

"The consignorii will disown and kill you for this, won't they?" Liat says.

I look over at the bruised and broken Bruse. "Yes."

Liat sits down on a purple padded wooden chair in front of a mirror lit by tens of small, wavering candles. "You could come with us. We need older allies to guide us through the countryside. You have talents we don't, you could share them, we could share with you. We are of all ages, and come from all over Elkatoa before we were taken to the factories. Our leader, Gull, she was once a captive of the Sea People. She doesn't lord over us, we're all free, together. We just want to get away from the city and try and start a small village of our own. We don't care about your past. You can bring your brother…"

It is an offer that brings with it a sliver of hope. Since the Sea People took their beachhead, since the allies of Habesh dallied at the foothills of Mount Oribeas to wait and see how strong the Sea People really were as they dashed themselves against the walls, I've thought of my fate as tied to the city and the consignorii.

Maybe there is another way.

Liat takes my hand and looks at me with a depth of seriousness that no child should have, but all in Habesh do. "I will get our Healer to come help Bruse. We will be leaving the city tonight, at midnight, by the old King's Road."

"You shouldn't have told me that," I say softly. "I knew where you would leave, but now I know when. The consignorii could take that from me. Or I could betray you."

She nods. "That's true. But I've looked into your mind, Jazim, and you are not nearly the horrible thing you make yourself out to be. I have faith you will do right by us, because the reason you've done these things you have is to protect those like us, and your brother. Not because you have a wicked heart. You strip away our magic so that we don't use it up, like Bruse, and end up used and begging on the streets. Not just because the consignorii manipulate you to do so."

"I wouldn't be so sure…" I start to say as I look down at the thick carpet, unable to meet her piercing eyes. Until now, people have always feared me. Here is a child who forgives and understands me.

Liat gets up and stands in front of me. "Go and get your brother. But be careful. You know what you'll have to do to bring him with us."

And then she hugs me. Like a little sister, wrapping her arms around my stomach before she turns to leave.

Outside, on the street, my mind is heavy with a black pall, and so is the sky.

THE CITY is like a man who takes his last meal the night before his execution. People are dancing in the streets, drunk and fearful. People are slinking in the shadows, trying to escape. People are grimly preparing for war, sharpening blades, dousing their rooftops with water, and hammering their windows shut.

In the squares, the Patriots are preparing the city for its stand.

They are tall, proud men with booming voices that make your insides quiver. They are illusions, these particular mouthpieces of the consignorii, much like the women of the Tannery district.

Here they stand, defiant against the Sea People invasion. "What manner of men are the Sea People?" they shout. "Inferior ones! Habesh is the greatest city on the coast of Elkatoa!" And they whip the crowd into pride and mania with great flashes of blue.

An orgiastic chant of 'Habesh, Habesh, Habesh' rises up to meet the pall of smoke over the city.

"They have raped our lands, raped our children, and raped our warriors in Kopach. They claim they want access to the forests, for their *ships*, and their *villages*." The speakers spit these words. "But we know what they want. Rape, pillage, destruction. They are *animals* who would imprison us, and rip from us our talents! Only Habeshi are the true children of the All. And it is Habeshi who will drive the Sea People back into the ocean where they belong. Brothers, we *will* fight! We will destroy! We will win! Join the defense of the walls *now*!"

The intensity rocks me, even passing the edge of a square in a hurry, and I find myself brimming with the desire to destroy the Sea People.

But I manage to regain control, and leave the raging crowds behind, even as hundreds surge to join the Guard and pick up a sword.

I force a vendor into giving me a meat pie and a flask of wine, and take both with me up the long winding stairs. The thick wooden door stands before me, with sunset an hour away.

"Jazim, is that you?" the frail voice of my brother asks from the other side. He has heard my footsteps.

"Yes," I say, my hand against the large brass knob.

A clink of metal inside. "The Sea People are close, aren't they? I can hear it down below on the street: they're saying a great defense of the walls is planned. Jazim. The speakers are out in the squares. Jazim. Please. You have to let me go help them. The city needs me. Let me help, please, brother, please."

It is like my soul is being cleaved.

"Listen," I whisper. "I...know a way we can leave the city..."

There is a silence for a long moment. A hush before the storm. A tear leaks from me, then I jump as a body slams against the door.

"You filthy excuse of Habeshi. Traitor. Heretic!" the voice on the other side screams, and I drop the flask of wine. It shatters, red liquid pooling around my boots, then bleeding down the stairs. "It is the lowest ebb of the tide of Habesh, but like a tide we will come rushing back and sweep them back where they belong."

I am wobbly, breathless, and shaken. He is right. There is a natural order to these things.

"Just because it is hard, doesn't mean one shouldn't do it!" the voice screams.

True. Many have thrown themselves against the walls of Habesh. And there is no greater folly than running whenever something looks hard.

He is right, my brother, I think as the faint blue sparkles of magic around the door fade away.

I open the door.

It is full of shadows, this room, but my brother shuffles out from them into the setting sunlight. The loose folds of his skin roll, and the giant, rheumy eyes regard me with hatred for my failings. The clink of his manacles fill the stony walls with echoes, and the chain drags along the dusty floor behind his left leg. It is a limb almost withered away, the life sucked out of it like the life had been taken from the rest of his body.

How much has he given to the city, for how long? And how has he survived this long?

His pride leads me to serve the consignorii. Puts me out of the tower every day with vigor. My brother: I love him almost as much as the city.

And he loves me back so dearly.

He rips the meat pie away from me, and gums at it with a messy sigh of contentment. "We must have our strength for the invasion," he mutters. "This city is the most beautiful thing in the world, and we must not let it be destroyed."

"We must have our strength to do the things we must," I say. I walk over to the balcony and look out over my city.

What did it mean to do the best thing for the city? Should I go back to capture the children? How long can we survive against the Sea People?

"You must let me out," my brother pleads. "Free me, let me go down to the squares. I will help others find their love of the city. Just like old days, brother, when I walked along the wall and gave courage and strength and pride to the defenders of Habesh."

I'm struggling with a chain of logic. For an hour ago, my mind had been in a vastly different place.

My brother loves me.

And I love him.

He is dying. The city is at ebb. What is my brother killing himself by using up the last of his life going to add to all this?

Nothing. He has almost no life left to give.

I love my city, but I love my brother too, almost as much. And I have the strength to do something I've needed to do for a long time.

I turn back from the balcony, my fingers tingling, and he opens his mouth. "Jazim?"

"Hadim...I love you..."

I'm sobbing as I rip his magic from him. He collapses to the ground, shocked, and I catch him. His body is tiny, frail, and his skin loose. His large, drooping eyes stare at me in confusion.

"I'm so sorry," I cry as I carry him to the cot by the wall.

I'm a wretched heretic, the consignorii will kill me the next time they see me. My brother will hate me.

But he will live.

Maybe the city will too.

I hope the children do not wait too long for me. If they had ever planned to do so.

IT IS past the sunset. In the distance the night is lit by massive approaching fires, their orange flare reflected off the bottom of gray, foreboding clouds.

The Sea People are at the walls.

The ground shakes with their march, and the impact of their projectiles.

My swords are at my side as I leave the tower filled with an incredible love for my fellow Habeshi who stand to fight. I see the city with my brother's eyes: an ancient edifice to all that is great about this coast. The place where all eventually end up, even the Sea People are drawn here.

Is there any greater place in the world than Habesh?

I think not.

This glorious city, this citadel on the coast where you can find anything you wish, buy anything you want. Here is where destinies are made, and stories created. Where lives are lived and legends made.

Yes, I think, as I prepare to join the defense of the wall, Habesh, you beautiful stinking whore of a city: I love you so.

The Stranger

L. E. MODESITT

*W*hen Patrick asked me if I'd be interested in contrib-
uting a story to Speculative Horizons, my immediate response
was, "Yes!" Then, after that instinctive and perhaps rash and
excessively rapid agreement, I had to think about what tale I wanted
to tell, since I didn't have a particular story in mind. I decided on
a Recluce story, if after a gentle hint or two by Patrick, and then
pondered over those characters who intrigued readers but who only
played small parts in any of the Recluce books to decide which one
might provide greater insight into the Saga for those who have read
it and interest those readers who have not read my work. In the
end, I found myself with "The Stranger," a story set, for those
who are interested, in the years immediately following The Chaos
Balance and roughly contemporaneous with Arms-Commander.
The stranger of the story is an unusual man, as much as for what
he does not say as for what he does say and do. For that reason,
what happens is told not from his viewpoint, but from that of someone whose life he changes forever through the events of just two

days. Some readers may see a parallel to a certain classic American western movie, but that parallel is only superficial, because the stranger of this story cannot ever forget from where he has come.

❖

*T*he late light oozed over the hills at the foot of the Easthorns that harvest afternoon, a light that gave the early snows on the higher peaks to the east the faintest tinge of orange. I heard the hoof-beats on the lane before I saw the man ride out of the sunset toward the cot and the sheep shed. I had just closed the door behind the flock. In those days, the mountain cats were far more numerous and far bolder, and any shepherd who left a flock outside was tempting fate. The fiercest of mastiffs were no match for a pair of cats. A young herder wasn't, either, and I was barely old enough to sprout a few hairs on my face. I also had no real weapons, just an iron-tipped staff and a belt dagger. Ma had sold the big old sword that had been Da's after he'd died when the Prefect had conscripted all the locals for an attack on Axalt. No one's ever breached the walls of the trading city, and the Prefect's forces didn't then, either. Ma got a death-gold, and that didn't even pay for the three lambs and the ewe that the armsmen took after they gave her the coin.

I glanced back at the shed for a moment. I was worried about the old ewe. She'd gone into season early in winter for the first time in a year, and the ram had covered her before we'd known, and she was showing signs her time was near.

Anyway, the hoof-beats got louder, and it was just before supper when the man rode up to the shed. He wore a black tunic, and black trousers, and even a black leather cloak. He wasn't young, and he wasn't old, but his face had the look of a man who'd traveled some. His hair was mahogany-red, but it didn't look that way then. In the sunset, it was more like the color of blood. He was also clean-shaven...or mostly so, like he'd shaved a day or two before.

"Young fellow, might a man find a hearth and a meal here?"

I didn't understand his words at first.

He asked again, and he spoke slowly. I still had to struggle to understand him because he spoke the way the traders from Suthya did, not quite the same, but close enough. What they called the old way of talking, sort of the way they did in Cyador, Caetyr told me later.

"We're not an inn, ser."

He smiled, sort of shyly. "I wasn't looking for an inn. I was looking for honest folk who wouldn't mind a few coppers for sharing their meal and letting a stranger sleep. I'd even sleep in the loft of the shed."

By then, Ma had come out into the yard. She just looked at him.

He turned in the saddle and bowed his head to her for a moment. "Mistress, I was asking the young fellow about whether I might pay you for a meal and a place to sleep."

"One way or the other, I'm no mistress." She paused. "There's an inn in town."

"A stranger traveling alone is often safer with honest herders." He smiled, and it was sort of a sad smile.

"That'd be so in places."

"And you're closer to Axalt. That's where I'm headed."

"You said you'd pay?" asked Ma.

"I did. Three coppers? Would that suffice?"

"We've only got a thick soup and fresh bread. No ale, nothing like that. Water's good, though. We got a clean spring backside of the hill."

"A thick soup would be wonderful." When he dismounted, I saw that he had two swords at his belt, both on the right side, and both sheathed in something like double scabbard, and a long dagger on his left side. The two swords were short blades, like nothing I'd ever seen. It was more than warm, but he wore a dark gray leather glove over his right hand, the kind that extended part way up his forearm under the sleeve of his tunic.

He slipped his wallet from his belt and deftly slid out three coppers one-handed, extending them to Ma.

"I guess you're our guest," Ma said with a smile.

"I thank you." He glanced toward the shed. "Might there be a place to put my mare? She's carried me more kays than I'd want to count."

"There's a large stall at the end of the shed," Ma said. "She'll have to share."

"She's done that before."

His horse was a black mare, and she did fine in with the old gelding. He groomed her with a worn brush that had leather straps that fitted over his gloved hand, and before long the three of us were sitting at the old table by the hearth.

Ma dished out the soup. She even used the better bowls and set the bread in a basket in the middle of the table.

"Would you like to say a blessing?" she asked.

"If you wouldn't mind...mine's a little different."

"A blessing's a blessing," Ma said warmly.

He cleared his throat gently before he spoke. "May we all live in order and peace, and may that order keep chaos and evil at bay. May we always understand the goodness of order and the perils of chaos, and live so that others do also, and may we always strive for the goodness that order brings, both for ourselves and others."

"That's a good blessing," Ma said. "Different, but good."

"You talk like you're from the west," I said.

"I'm from a place called Carpa. It's in Lornth." He broke his bread one handed, with his left hand. I watched him for a moment. He didn't use his right hand at all.

He looked at me. "You're very observant. My right hand was hurt years ago. I can do some things with it, but eating's not one of them."

Ma gave me a look. So I asked, "Where have you been lately?"

"I was in Passera a while ago."

"That's two eightday's ride," Ma said.

"I didn't ride it. I came downriver to Elparta on a flatboat. It took four days." He shook his head. "It might have been better to ride."

"It take you a long time to get here from Carthan?" I asked.

"Carpa." He laughed, soft-like. "Ten years or so."

"Lornth is beyond the Westhorns. Did you see the ones they call Angels when you came east?"

"I have seen them," the man said.

"Are they six cubits high with silver hair and eyes, the way they say?"

He laughed, again. "Some have silver hair. I saw one who had silver eyes. None was taller than four and a half cubits, perhaps not that."

"There must be a lot of them."

"There were only thirty or so who came from the Rational Stars. That's what they told me, and they don't lie."

"All folks lie at times," Ma said.

"They don't bother with it. At least, the ones I knew didn't."

"They're all women, aren't they?" That was what I'd heard.

"Most of them. Not all. One was a black mage, and a smith. His name was Nylan. He could bend the fires of heaven and draw something even hotter from a simple charcoal forge. He hammered out blades there on the Roof of the World that could cleave through the best iron in Candar. He forged other things, too." The stranger's eyes got a faraway look in them for a moment.

"What about the women?" I asked.

"Frankyr…" Ma said that in her quiet voice, the one that told me I was being rude.

"They were warriors, like no one in Candar has ever seen before, even more skilled and deadly than the fabled Mirror Lancers of ancient Cyador. I watched the one they called the marshal, Ryba of the Swift Ships of Heaven. She was tall for a woman, almost as tall as I am. With nothing but a pair of short blades she killed three Lornian armsmen and sliced off the sword hand of a fourth in less time than it takes to tell it." He shook his head. "Folks don't believe me when I say that, but it's true."

"Those short blades the kind you have?"

He looked at me. "They are. They were forged by Nylan."

"They don't seem very big, not like the sword Da had."

"They're very good, especially for close fighting on horseback. They can also be thrown. Saryn of the black blades could throw one hard enough that it would pierce a breastplate and the point would come out through a man's back."

"You saw that?"

"Once." The stranger nodded, then stood. "I thank you for the supper, and I'll be headed out to the loft."

I watched him from the side of the cot, but he did pretty much what he said he'd do. Then I walked back inside and barred the door.

Ma looked at me. She was still sitting on the bench. "He's a strange man. I think he's a good one, though."

"Someone must be chasing him," I said. "Why would he want to stay here? What he gave you would almost pay for a meal and bed at the inn."

"He's not a common armsman," Ma said.

"With all that black, you think he's an assassin or a bravo?"

"He might have been...before he hurt his hand." She shook her head. "He doesn't swagger."

"Maybe he was a captain or an undercaptain."

"He doesn't want to say...but he's not common."

Neither one of us said what we were thinking—that with his weapons and his skills, he could have taken anything he wanted. In the time before I dropped off to sleep, I wondered why he'd avoided the town.

The next morning, once we opened the door, it wasn't long before the stranger appeared. He'd brushed his clothes clean. He must have found the spring, because he was washed up, and he'd shaved. Cleaned-up, he looked a little younger, but I'd have guessed he was still more than ten years older than me, but not so old as Ma.

She offered him maybe a quarter of a loaf, and he gave her a copper, then stood on the stoop and ate the bread with water from the mug Ma offered.

"You led armsmen, didn't you?" Ma asked.

He finished eating before he answered. "I did. I have to admit I wasn't too successful. I haven't done that in years."

"What are you doing here in Spidlar?"

"Like I told you last night, I'm passing through on my way to Axalt. There's no way to get there from Passera without crossing the Easthorns and then crossing them back—except through Spidlar."

Ma looked at me. "You'd best take the flock before it gets too hot."

I wanted to hear what the stranger might say, but Ma was right, and I took the iron-tipped staff that had been Da's and headed out to the shed. I didn't worry about the stranger. Maybe I should have, but there was something about him. Besides, if he'd meant harm, he'd already have done it, and with those blades of his, I couldn't have stopped him. I did look back a couple of times, but by the time I'd reached the hilltop with the flock, he was walking back to where his mare was stalled.

We hadn't grazed the hills to the southwest in a time, and that was where I headed, with the old ram and me leading the way. The grass there wasn't bad, but it was browning earlier than it usually did, and that meant we'd likely have a dry summer, an early winter, and a long one.

When I brought the flock back in late afternoon, Ma and the stranger were out by the shed, and there was a pile of coal there piled against the west wall, tall as he was and four times that far across. I don't know as I'd ever seen that much coal in one place before that.

"Where did all this coal come from?" With all that coal we wouldn't be hoarding wood and scraps and freezing, the way we had the winter before. That was if we were careful, but it looked like it would last a while.

"I was walking up in the hills, and I saw a few little pieces in the dry wash, and I started following them." The stranger shrugged. "I showed your mother where the seam comes out. I wouldn't tell anyone. Someone would just come and take the land and the coal."

"It's our land."

"That may be, but unless you've got golds to hire armsmen or you're armsman trained, you'll lose it to those who have coin or weapons. Coal that good's worth a shiny silver."

"That's not right."

"Was it right that your father got conscripted to attack Axalt?"

I didn't answer for a moment. Ma had been talking. I hadn't said anything about Da. I looked at her and then at him and wondered what else might have been happening.

"Nothing," he answered, as if he'd been able to hear my thoughts. "The mare needs another day of rest. I rode her too hard getting here. That was because I thought I could reach Axalt yesterday."

"He spent all day walking up to where he found the coal, chipping it out, and putting it in bags for the gelding to carry back. It took all day," Ma said. "Then he washed up."

I didn't say anything.

"It's going to be a long, cold winter," he said.

The way he said that was not like he guessed, but that he *knew*.

"You didn't have to do that," I told him.

"The world would be a pretty sorry place if we only did what we had to, don't you think?" he replied.

I'd heard words like that before. Seeing him standing there, with the one hand still gloved in gray, and looking at a pile of coal it would have taken me days to lug anywhere, what he said sounded different. He hadn't just said the words. He'd said them after he'd done something to show that he meant them.

I just stared at him, because I didn't know what to say and because Ma was looking at me with a disgusted expression on her face.

"Someone's coming." He turned toward the lane from town, quicker than a mountain cat. "Get in the cot."

Ma looked at him.

"Inside." His words were so powerful that I grabbed Ma by the arm and dragged her back to the stoop. But we didn't go in. We stood half in and half out of the doorway watching.

Four men on horses trotted up the lane, fast enough that the dust billowed almost to the girths of their saddles. The stranger stood there, halfway between the cot and the sheep shed, waiting, like he knew them.

Two of the riders were big men, maybe not quite so tall as the stranger in black, but broader across the shoulders. The third rider was smaller, and even from where we were, he looked mean, with a slash scar across one cheek, and a lash in his right hand. The last rider waited behind the other two. He wasn't big, and he wasn't small, and he wore a shoulder harness with two blades in it.

The stranger didn't say anything. The first three riders reined up some fifteen yards away from where he stood.

"You won't be getting away this time!" called the big rider in the middle. He had a big blade out, laid across his thighs for the moment.

The one on the right also had a big blade. He just smirked.

"You don't want to do this," the stranger replied. "I'm leaving Gallos. You could turn around and leave."

"After chasing you for hundreds of kays?" The one with the whip laughed. "We're here to get our golds." He paused. "Unless you'd like to pay more than the Prefect will."

He lifted the whip hand, and I could see that the butt of the weapon was fastened around his wrist with leathers. I guessed that was so he didn't lose it.

The stranger was the one to laugh. "You're not that honest. If I gave you golds you'd cheerfully take them and then still try to take me."

"Hear that," said the one in the middle. "The teacher fellow doesn't think we're honest. Teach us something, teacher fellow."

All three of them laughed.

When the laughs died away, the stranger spoke, and his voice filled the yard. He wasn't shouting. His words just carried. "No one can teach you. No one can teach another anything unless the listener wants to learn. I can speak, but you cannot learn if you will not find the order within yourselves."

The three front riders all laughed again.

While they were laughing, the stranger did nothing...except somehow, he seemed *blacker*, darker, more solid. And he had a blade in his left hand. It looked real small compared to the ones that the two big men on horseback held.

"I guess we'll be doing the teaching, then," said the middle rider, looking to the rider with the lash. The four rode forward a way and then stopped.

The man with the whip flicked it in the direction of the stranger, and it cracked just short of him.

The stranger didn't move.

"The teacher fellow wants us to think he's brave," said the big man in the middle. "Roart, see how brave he really is."

The whip lashed out at the stranger, but it didn't strike him, but wound around his short blade. Then he jerked and turned or something, and the rider with the whip was pulled right out of the saddle, and one boot caught in the stirrup for a moment, and then he arched into the air and came down on his head. Hard. He didn't move, and it didn't look like he would. Ever.

The other three froze for a moment.

Then the lead rider lifted his blade and spurred his horse forward. The horse barely had taken three strides when I saw a black blade sticking out of the man's chest.

The remaining rider of the front three charged the stranger. My mouth was open as the second black blade buried itself in that bravo's chest. At that moment the stranger started to move toward the big blade that had dropped from the hands of the man who'd done most of the talking.

I ran from the door because I could see that the stranger wouldn't get to the blade before the last rider did. The rider looked to be a Kyphran nomad. The staff wasn't much against a big blade, but it was the only thing I had. Ma tried to grab me, but she was too slow.

The Kyphran was already swinging one of those hand-and-a-half swords when he rode toward the stranger, who was still crouching, because he'd had to dig the fallen blade out of a rut in the yard. The rider was already by me, but I took the staff and lunged, and I swung it at the back of his sword arm and hit him as hard as I could. The blade flew clear, and he turned the horse and pulled out another blade almost as big as the first.

"You're going to be sorry for that, boy." The bravo cut down at me.

I got the old staff up in time to keep that blade from going through me, and it stopped the blade and held. My legs didn't, and I sprawled on the ground, and when I hit, I lost hold of the staff. Then I tried to scramble out of the way.

The bravo came back and was bringing his sword down, when he got this funny look on his face, and then slumped forward in the saddle. His head lolled a funny way, and then the horse stopped, and he fell face-first out of the saddle and into the dirt.

The stranger was standing on the other side of the horse, and he already had the reins in his left hand, and the big blade of the other bravo—that was the one he must have used—was lying in the dirt.

It took me a moment to climb to my feet. When I did, the stranger handed me the reins. "Can you tie this horse up in the pen by the shed?"

"Yes, ser." I don't know why I called him "ser," but it seemed right.

I started to walk the big courser toward the pen, but I looked back to see where the other three horses were. The one that was the farthest away—he was almost a hundred yards south—he had this wild look that I saw even from where I was.

The stranger turned toward the wild-eyed horse. Then he called, "Here, fellow." Demon-flame if the big horse didn't stop and sort of snort and snuffle before he began to walk toward the stranger. He did that with the other mounts, and before long, we had them all four tied up in the pen beside the sheep shed.

Ma had been out in the yard for a time, looking at the four dead men, then at the horses tied in the pen, then at stranger, and finally at me. "You shouldn't have done it with the staff, Frankyr. You could have been killed."

"No, if you'd done the careful thing, you shouldn't have," said the stranger as he fastened the gate to the pen, "but careful isn't always right. I'm glad you did the right thing. Otherwise, things might have turned out differently, for all of us." He turned to Ma. "I'm sorry about all this. I didn't think they'd be able to track me here."

"That why you took the flatboat downriver?" asked Ma.

"I hoped they'd leave me alone." He shrugged. "I should have known better, but I tried not to have things turn out this way."

"This way?" Ma's voice wasn't cutting, but it had a touch of the edge she put on the words when she didn't believe me.

"The killing. I don't like killing, for all that I once tried to gain a holding by it. It didn't work out. That taught me something, and I've tried to avoid it ever since." He took a deep breath. "The problem is that, sometimes, when you try to avoid something too much, it's like you draw it to you."

"So how did not wanting to kill draw these fellows after you?" Ma gestured at the bodies, but she didn't look at them.

"I left Westwind and the Roof of the World after the great battle where Nylan destroyed the flower of Lornth, and I headed east. I've been in Gallos for a while, telling people about order and how it works." He stopped and looked hard at me. "Most young people don't understand. I didn't, not until I ran into the angels. But that's another story. Anyway…it's like this. Rulers all tell a story, and it's usually a story that makes them look good. If they know people won't believe that story, then they talk about how evil someone else is and how everything they do causes the problems folks have. Once I was one of those who believed the stories. That was before the angels came, and I watched and listened to the great mage Nylan. He showed me how the world really is. The funny thing was that he didn't like to be called a mage. Said he was something called an engineer on a ship that sailed between the stars. I wouldn't have believed that, either, once. Anyway… I've been traveling and telling people what little I've learned from the angels. The new prefect of Gallos didn't care for my teaching, because he's been trying to tell the story that all the problems in Gallos, maybe everywhere in Candar, have been caused by the angels. The angels live in a tower—one black stone tower on the Roof of the World. It's high and cold, where no one ever lived before. They never left the Westhorns until they were attacked, both by Lornth and Gallos. For all that little more than a double handful of them slaughtered two mighty armies, they never left the Roof of the World, even after those triumphs. So how can they have caused all these problems? A handful of people on top of the Westhorns who just want to be left alone?" The stranger laughed, sort of ruefully. "The new prefect didn't like my telling people that. His armsmen came and burned the Temple I'd built in Passera. It wasn't very big, but it was where I was telling people about order. I wasn't there at the time. That made him so mad that he put a price on my head."

"For telling folks what was really happening?"

"Well…" The stranger smiled sheepishly. "I did fight off a couple of armsmen who tried to capture me and take me to Fenard so that I could be drawn and quartered. One of them died, I think, but I didn't stay to find out. I thought that, if I left Passera, there wouldn't be any need for them to kill me or me to kill them in order to stay alive. The Prefect didn't like that. I was charged with treason for pointing out that the way of the angels brought down great Cyador and defeated the forces of both Gallos and Lornth. So I thought I'd best leave Gallos. But they sent a whole squad of armsmen to block the road east of Passera. It seemed like a better idea to take the river north and head for Axalt this way. Otherwise I'd have to go through Certis, and the ruler there is friendly to the Prefect, while Axalt has no love of him."

Ma and I knew that.

Suddenly, he cocked his head, then stood and hurried toward the sheep shed. There, he unbarred the door and slipped inside. I hurried after him, and so did Ma, after she ran inside the cot and came back out with the lantern.

The old ewe was against the wall of the shed, and the others had given her space.

"She's not going to make it," Ma said. "I can tell."

The stranger knelt down on the soiled straw, close to the ewe, and she let him. I don't know what he did, but one moment, the old ewe was bleating in distress, and he put his left hand on her head, and it stopped. Then he began to talk to her like she was a sick child, and this black mist…or something like it… blacker than the darkness in the places where the light from the lantern couldn't reach…it sort of ran down his good arm and into the ewe.

Ma and I just watched.

He didn't seem to do anything, and yet he did.

It must have been a good glass that passed while she delivered the two lambs…and the afterbirth. He touched both of the newborns somehow with that blackness, and before long, both lambs were nursing, and the old ewe was acting years younger, like nothing at all had been wrong.

When the stranger stood and turned, so that the light from the lantern fell on his face, he looked older, worn-out, a lot more tired than after he'd fought the men who'd been chasing him, and his face was all sweaty. "They should be all right now."

"What did you do? You some kind of mage?" asked Ma, so soft that I could tell she was half scared and half plain shocked.

"I'm no mage, not the way the angels are. I couldn't topple mighty Cyador and make the whole world shudder. I've just learned a few things along the way." He looked at me. "Anyone can learn some things about order." He shook his head. "We still need to get rid of the bodies. If they're found around here, you'll be the ones blamed."

"They tried to kill you…" I began.

"That doesn't matter. Anyone who helps a traitor is guilty, and I don't think you want to be hung or leave everything and head for Axalt." He looked at Ma.

She shook her head. "I'll get the spade."

We walked outside, and Ma hurried to the cot and then back with the spade and sort of thrust it at the stranger's right hand.

He wasn't looking and the shaft struck his glove. It sort of *clunked*, dull-like, and he grabbed the shaft with his left hand. "I'm sorry. My right hand isn't that limber."

It didn't sound limber at all. It sounded like there was metal under the glove. I wondered if he had some sort of wrist guard or brace there, but before I could ask, he said, "We'll need to use the gelding to carry the bodies, one at a time. Can you do that, Frankyr, while your mother shows me somewhere over the hill where we can bury them?"

"Yes, ser."

We finished burying the four of them on the far side of the hill sometime before midnight. The stranger insisted that we dig deep, and he and I did the digging while Ma held the lantern.

He gave us all the coins that the strangers had, and there were fifteen coppers and five silvers, and one plain gold ring. "You could have gotten that anywhere. I'd not sell it for a season or so, though, just to be safe."

Then, after we stalled the gelding, he saw us to the cot and walked back to the shed. I heard him climb up to the loft.

When I woke just after first light and went out to offer him breakfast, he was gone. So were the four horses. There was a cloth pouch tied to the bar on the inside of the sheep shed, with six golds inside, and a scrap of parchment with words written on it.

I'd never been to school, and I couldn't read what he wrote. Ma couldn't either, but the golds spoke for themselves, and who could we have asked to read it right then? Years later, when no one was asking about the riders who disappeared, when I went to Axalt to sell some sheep, I had a merchant there read it to me, and he said that it read:

You and your mother deserve half.

Remember—believe in order, and live in order, and all will be right.

Under the words was just a letter. I could tell that. It was an "R."

I guess we follow order. Anyway, I tried. A good herder might bring in a gold a year, and we had six. So we spent a few silvers here and few there for a good ram or ewe, and before long Ma could buy a loom, and one thing led to another.

The one thing that bothered me, and it still does, is that we never even knew his name. I suppose we didn't need to. The lambs grew into strong ewes, and they lived twice as long as any we ever had. They also stayed black, and so did all their lambs, and the lambs that came from them, and we get twice as much for their wool. That's how we could build a real house here and buy more of the land. We've kept the coal to ourselves, though.

You might say that all that came from the blackness of a good-hearted stranger.

Flint

BRIAN RUCKLEY

*N*ow and again I get hooked on some random aspect of history. It's like contracting an obscure airborne virus: I go to bed perfectly normal, and wake up the next morning with an insatiable desire to know more about the Byzantine Empire, or the Korean War, or Ancient Greece.

In this case, it was prehistoric hunter-gatherers. So I read a bit about how our species lived before some bright spark came up with the idea of farming, and I was taken by the idea that these were cultures as alien and unfamiliar to us pampered moderns as any invention of a fantasy author. Inevitably, rather than just enjoying the experience of reading and thinking about those distant times and lives, I did what most writers do when confronted with new knowledge, and started looking for ways to squeeze stories out of it. We can never just leave things alone. It's an affliction.

This story didn't need much squeezing, though. The basic idea came very quickly: a Stone Age in which magic was real, and loosely based on the shamanic beliefs of our own past. Even the

*central character's name – Flint – offered itself up almost at once,
and just stuck.*

*But I didn't write Flint's story down. It sat there, half-formed,
in my head; filed away on the dusty mental shelf where you keep
stuff you don't have time to knock into shape. It waited there for
months and months and months, and it never really stopped being
my favourite of all the short story ideas I had stored away.*

*And then, as I was drawing near to the end of the big fan-
tasy trilogy that had taken up all my writing time for so long,
an invitation arrives, out of the blue. Like a little piece of luck,
fluttering across the tubes of the internet. Would I care to contribute a story to an anthology?, a certain fellow called Pat
enquires. Why yes, I would. There's this shaman, called Flint,
who, as it turns out, has been waiting for someone to ask that
very question ...*

*T*he sky, above: eggshell-blue, strewn with lines of cloud
like unmoving waves on an inverted sea.

The real sea, beneath: lazy in the heat, rubbing itself up
against the pebble beach. Sifting the stones.

The shaman, Flint: considering whether to intervene in order
to preserve this tranquillity.

FATHEAD WAS squatting down, defecating, on the far side of the
midden. Flint could only see the back of his head, poking up
beyond the sprawling heap of mussel shells and bones and broken tools and stone chips. Mouse was stalking Fathead, creeping

through the small cluster of deerhide shelters. He had a smooth, beach-scavenged stone in his hand.

Flint sat cross-legged amongst the stunted bushes on the bank behind the camp, watching the stalk in silence. Mouse was a small boy, and Fathead's skull was thick. Even a well-flighted stone would do no lasting harm. But there would be anger, and noise, and strife: a delight for Mouse, whose happiness fed upon such things; annoyance for Flint, who was trying to die, at least a little, and needed all his concentration.

EVERYONE ELSE, except the ailing Long Dusk, was down on the shore gathering shellfish. Fathead remained in the camp to watch over Long Dusk. He was too slow and dull to be of much other use. Mouse, having hidden until his mother gave up searching for him, remained to torment Fathead. Flint remained because the others did not want him on the beach with them. Some of them doubted he was ready for the mantle of shaman, and they were not yet sure whether he brought them good or ill luck. They probably feared his presence might sour any shellfish that were gathered, and turn them foul in the guts of those who ate them.

Flint churred out a rattling hiss, a grasshopper's sharp song. Mouse paused, looked towards him. There was irritation, and a flutter of something much harder and fiercer, on the younger boy's face. Flint frowned and flicked his head.

Mouse bared his teeth in fleeting defiance, but Flint was older by three or four summers and that—along with his newly acquired standing as shaman, however fragile—was enough. Mouse dropped the stone and scurried away through the scattered shelters, heading for the beach. Fathead, oblivious, was grunting in self-absorbed satisfaction.

Flint breathed out slowly and evenly. Closed his eyes. Turned his attention to the matter of a small death. He only wanted to go partway; just enough to let things show through. For that, with luck, he would need no powders or brews. No preparatory fast, no chants, no dance. No Hare. That last would be good, if he could manage it. Hare's manner was not always as supportive as it might have been.

Flint separated himself from the feel of the sun's heat on his skin, and from the press of grass and hard earth against his hide-clad thighs and buttocks. He gathered the weight of his body and the weave of his thoughts into his chest and breathed them out, bit by bit. Eventually, there was so little of him left that his spirit came unfixed from his flesh and he hung there, formless, in the borderland between the two worlds: the shallow, in which his body sat cross-legged amongst the scrub and the birdsong, and the deep, in which there was light and shade, pattern and flow.

He let his spirit drift along the edge of the deep and secret world, drawing nearer to the shadow of Long Dusk's sickness. It was like a bruise of smoke before him, and beneath it, at its root, was Long Dusk herself, or her spirit form at least: an indistinct shape, vaguely womanly, formed of shimmering soul-stuff.

'What are you doing?'

Flint did not turn around. He knew the voice all too well, merriment and scepticism and curiosity all shoaling within it like so many jostling fish.

'I want to see what is wrong with Long Dusk,' Flint said.

'Is she sick?' Hare moved closer, into Flint's line of sight. Here in the place that was neither one thing nor the other, Hare had no clear shape; he was an idea, an outline.

'Yes,' Flint said. 'As soon as we got here, she fell sick. But Rope-in-Hand has told me to stay away. Says the women can care for their own. Says a squab like me is no use for this sort of thing.'

'Oh. Squab? A little scrawny, perhaps, but squab is rather hurtful.' Hare sounded mildly offended on Flint's behalf. But he also sounded amused. 'Was she in a particularly bad mood when she said that?'

Flint grunted. Hare was distracting him, and it was getting harder to hold his awareness in place. He still could not see Long Dusk clearly enough to tease out any knowledge. Surely, he thought, not for the first time, a shaman's guide was supposed to offer aid rather than hindrance?

'I can help,' Hare duly said, with great eagerness. 'I could go deeper; see if Long Dusk's spirit will talk to me. Ask it what ails her. Oh, or we could travel to one of the Owl Fathers. They always know what to do, in matters of sickness. Although the last time I met one, he snagged fur from my back with a talon. Never knew whether that was a mistake or not.'

'There is no need,' Flint said blandly. 'I will just take a look at her from here. See what I can see.'

'No need,' the spirit guide sniffed. 'A shaman with no need for his guide. Fifth Moon didn't teach you such ideas. He was a true shaman, a walker of many paths, a man of—'

'I know he was. And I do need you. Just not now, not for this.'

Flint concentrated, and encouraged Long Dusk's blighted spirit to take on the features of her fleshly body. He could see her blunt nose, her eyebrows like old furry caterpillars, the weathered nut-brown skin of her cheeks. Skin that moved, as if stretched this way and that by a restless tongue beneath. But Flint did not think it was her tongue shifting and probing in the pit of her mouth. He allowed himself to sink still closer to her, so close that he was breathing the murk of her sickness. He heard, coming from behind her teeth, a flat and droning insectile hum, and he saw, quivering at the corner of her mouth, a tiny twig of a leg poking out for a moment between her lips.

'Ah.' Flint said.

'Ah what?' asked Hare. Flint could feel his guide edging nearer, mastered by curiosity.

'I see you,' Flint said.

'See what?' Hare asked. 'Who are you talking to?'

Flint said nothing more. He opened himself to his senses; let himself feel the warmth, hear the birds in the scrub, smell the sweet scent the sun was sweating out of the flowers. He flowed back towards himself.

'Wait,' he heard Hare muttering, a little petulant, a little pained. 'Wait! What did you see? Did we learn something?'

And then Flint was entirely alive again, his body and spirit one, and Hare was gone. He was sitting once more on the bank behind the camp, looking down towards the shelter in which Long Dusk lay dying.

THE REST of them came up from the beach. Flint heard them, crunching and chattering their way over the shingle, before he saw them, and could tell from their sound that they had done well. They carried willow baskets heavy with mussels and cockles, and piles of seaweed. All this bounty, and the warmth and easiness of the day, made them happy and loud. The children brandished fat crabs at one another, and shrieked. The men and the women laughed. They brought into the camp the smell of the sea, and of weed-draped rocks, and of airs carried from the far horizon on the back of waves.

Flint went down to meet the returning families, and one of the youngest girls—Dew-on-Grass—thrust a crab at him as if to nip him with its claws. He feigned alarm, and she ran off, delighted. The children had none of their parents' distrust of youth in a shaman. Nor did they care that those whose teachers fell foul of the spirits inherited a stain of misfortune.

Rope-in-Hand greeted him not with smiles or games but a tight scowl. Flint winced, fearing that she knew, somehow, of his disobedience to her instructions. But that was the child he had been not so long ago. The man, the shaman, he was striving to become steadied his features.

'Long Dusk is dying,' he said quietly as all about them the others dispersed, some to their shelters, some to set fires; the children to chase one another with still-writhing crabs.

Rope-in-Hand dropped her round basket of mussels to the ground. It thudded down, denting the sandy soil. She was stocky and heavy-browed. Her authority over the group, inarguable now that Fifth Moon was dead, flowed from a mixture of character, age and knowledge of a few charms and chants of the sort reserved to wise women.

'I told you not to interfere,' she growled at Flint.

'I only looked,' he muttered. He could hear, even now, the wheeze of Long Dusk's breath. It sounded, to Flint, like a terribly thin hold for anyone to have on life. 'But looking is enough to know that she is dying. Her sickness is a thing of the spirit world—'

Rope-in-Hand bunched her nose into a nest of wrinkles.

'You shamans think everything comes from the other world.'

Flint did not want to dislike Rope-in-Hand, but it was difficult to do anything else. After the father of her children died—never returning from a solitary hunt, victim of tooth or claw or tusk out in the wild woods that fringed this very shore—she had often shared nights, and the warmth of her body, with Fifth Moon. She had always paid Flint, his pupil, little heed, but her manner—not only towards Flint, but towards life as a whole—had roughened after Fifth Moon in his turn followed the ochre path.

'She will die,' Flint said stubbornly. 'I can help her. It is what I am supposed to do.'

'Even if you are right about where it comes from, playing shaman's games with sickness is not something for one as young as you. Fifth Moon died when he tried it, and he was much loved by the spirits. He had known them longer than you have lived.'

Bitterness sharpened her words. She had, Flint thought, not yet forgiven Fifth Moon for dying. Flint's teacher had indeed been taken by another's sickness: trying, and failing, to undo the fever burning in one of the children, he had himself fallen prey to whatever malign spirits lay behind it. But for all that Flint had valued Fifth Moon's guidance, he had never been blind to the man's flaws, a certain prideful incaution not least among them. He did not mean to repeat his predecessor's mistakes.

'But I have seen what it is that afflicts her,' he insisted.

'Leave this in the hands of the women. We will find other things for you to do, little shaman. Safer things. Things that will bring no harm down upon us if you fail in them.'

With that she picked up her basket and stomped away, leaving Flint to chew at his lip thoughtfully. He noticed Mouse leaning on the frame of a sealskin windbreak. While the other children squealed and squalled their way around the camp, caught up in their games, Mouse stared fixedly at Flint. His gaze was sharp with loathing. Flint had done nothing to earn the boy's dislike, but Mouse had far too much of the stuff stewing away inside him to reserve it only for those who earned it.

Flint turned away. His parents had died long ago. As a young child, he had shown little instinctive skill in things that mattered—hunting, making tools from the stone that gave him his name, working wood or hide. Until the spirits marked him as a future shaman and Fifth Moon, somewhat grudgingly, took him under his tutelary wing, Flint had been adrift. Now that he had found a place and purpose, he could not let Rope-in-Hand bar his way. He was a shaman. He believed he might be a good one, in time. All that remained was to convince everybody else of that.

He began to plan what he would need to take with him into the woods, if he was to save Long Dusk.

As FLINT walked, the grass grew softer and lusher beneath his feet, the oak trees twisted and turned their way higher, the air grew stiller. He went cautiously through the clearings and thickets and the stands of old trees, and kept his hand tight about his stone-bladed spear, since it was difficult to see far. Men died easily in forests.

An observer might have thought Flint's meandering path to be the result of an idle or inattentive mind; in fact, he followed his shaman's instincts, and the faint flavours of life and death and growth and change he could taste beneath the surface of the world. These things brought him to the shade of a fat, old oak that reached for the blue sky with a host of crooked arms.

Its shape was pleasing to Flint, and he thought that once it must have been a fine and wise tree. But there was rot in it now, opening a soft split in its trunk, flaking the bark away from the lower branches and turning the wood beneath brown. There were many gaps in the flock of leaves it extended towards the sun.

High up on the trunk, bees came and went from a ragged crevice. They hummed to and fro through the dappled pattern of shadows and sunlight that fell from the tree's canopy. The juices quickened in Flint's mouth at the thought of honey, but he put that greedy reflex aside. He had other business with the bees today.

He set a small fire at the base of the tree, feeding it with the sheddings of the oak and flavouring the smoke with dried marsh orchid flowers and scrapings from the roots of rushes. He fanned the rising tendrils of smoke into his face, drawing a little of it in through his nose. He whispered out long, soft promises of his benign intent and the smoke he exhaled carried them up. He closed his eyes. The fire crackled, and the smoke ascended. Flint tapped a quiet beat out with his fingertip on the tiny drum he carried. He put into that rhythm a gentle call, asking Hare to come to him.

Time let go of him—or he of it—so he could not be sure how long it took, but there came a moment when he had left his body behind and was standing in the spirit world, before an oak as tall and sturdy as any he had ever seen. This must be how the tree remembered itself, how it had been at the peak of its vigour. Some truths, though, could not be undone, and the mighty trunk was shot through with veins of decay that in this deeper world shone white as bleached whale bone. They sprang from somewhere amongst the tree's roots and climbed through its bole, spreading out along its boughs and up into its canopy.

'Hare,' Flint murmured. 'I need your help.'

This time, because Flint had crossed all the way, and entered entirely into the land of meaning, Hare appeared in his true form. He sat on his haunches in front of the shaman. His black-tipped ears reached almost as high as Flint's eyes; his lustrous gold-brown pelt shone as if brushed by sunlight, and shimmered as if stirred by a breeze. His long face, tipped with a twitching nose, wore a grave expression.

'You shouldn't be so rude to me.'

'Rude?'

'Disappearing back to the dull world like that, without any explanation. Not telling me what is happening, what you've seen. Fifth Moon wouldn't have done that. He understood how it should be, between a shaman and his guide.'

'I am sure he did. Fifth Moon evidently understood a great many things I do not.'

'Now that is a great big truth. Big and bright as the sun. Bigger, even. Brighter. Oh, it hurts my eyes just to look at that truth, it's so—'

'But still, he died,' Flint observed.

'Well, yes,' Hare said sulkily. 'It was very sad. I miss him.'

'He died,' said Flint, who did not miss Fifth Moon nearly as much as Hare did, 'and I became shaman in his place. That is what he taught me for.'

'Very sad,' Hare repeated morosely.

'I need your help now, though,' Flint said as brightly as he could. 'Will you ask the bees to speak with me?'

'Bees?' repeated Hare with a little peak of surprise and interest in his voice.

'They are in this tree.'

Hare regarded the scarred trunk before them. He ground his teeth together uneasily as he examined the pale tracery of decay.

'What's this?' he muttered. 'That's no ordinary ailment for a tree.'

'The bees could tell us,' Flint said.

Hare eyed him dubiously, but ascended into the branches, like a feather upon the wind's breath. He sat on a thick bough and pressed his eye against a hole in the tree's skin.

'Is this still about the woman's sickness?' he asked, shuffling about on his elevated perch as he tried to get a better view into the heart of the tree.

'It is. I saw—,'

But Flint's thought went unexpressed, for Hare abruptly shrank away from the cranny into which he had been peering, his eyes now wide, his ears snapping back to lie flat along his neck and spine.

'Run,' Hare yelped. 'Run, run, run.'

'But I want to talk to them,' Flint said as Hare tumbled away from the tree, so upset that he seemed to have forgotten how to fly.

'They don't want to talk to you,' Hare cried.

And with that, the tree gave forth a black fog that poured out from its heart, roaring as it came. Its countless tiny bodies seethed; its countless wings beat out a thunderous storm. It boiled up amongst the oak's branches and threw dark coils about them. Light failed.

Flint backed away, and instinctively began to form his thoughts into a shape that would return him to the shallower, and safer, world he had left behind.

Too late, though, for the cloud of bees made a great churning knot of itself up amongst the boughs, hung there for a moment, and then swept down towards him. He fell onto his back.

The bees took on a shape as their cold shadow laid itself over him. From their innumerable bodies they made one: a shifting, blunt-limbed guess at a human form.

'Oh,' said Flint, which sounded foolish even to his own ears.

'Get up!' he could hear Hare shouting, but fear had arrived to make him feeble and dull his thoughts.

The swarm extended a swirling mock arm and pinned Flint down. The deafening drone of it battered at his ears, and made his ribcage tremble. He could feel hatred and bitter anger beating at him, too. It was carried by the bees, but it did not belong to them. It belonged to the thing that had possessed them.

Before Flint could do anything with this new, dimly perceived understanding, the swarm leaned its featureless face close to his own, opened a dark pit of a mouth in its surface and fell upon him. He felt the brittle legs scrambling over his skin; he felt the wings rattling against his eyelids. The bees forced their way into his nose. They burrowed their way between his lips, and when he parted his teeth to try for a desperate breath, they flooded into his mouth and his throat. He could feel bees scraping down his windpipe and into his chest, and was unsure whether he would die or go mad first. His lungs seethed with coarse and quivering movement. Then there was sudden light, and Flint dared to open his eyes.

Hare, shining, burst through the furious swarm and broke it apart. It slumped out of its crude human shape. Its tendrils raspingly withdrew from Flint's nostrils and chest.

'Go back!' Hare was shouting. 'I'll lead them on a long dance, all the way to the Sunset Lands if need be.'

Hare sounded excited, but it was a strained, high kind of excitement, fed by danger. Flint rolled onto his side, then onto his hands and knees. He had no true flesh here, of course, yet still his lips, his tongue, the insides of his nose and throat, all felt as though they had been rubbed raw.

He gathered memories of the shallow world to him, and embraced them with heartfelt longing. He caught a final glimpse of Hare bounding into the bright distance, singing, with the storm of bees diving at his haunches, and then Flint was gone.

HE DUG into the earth at the base of the oak tree while the sinking sun looked on. Soft beams of evening light came low through the woodlands. Flint's spear, planted upright within easy reach, threw a long, straight shadow over the pit he excavated. A thin wash of sweat spread over his arms and his back. The damp soil crumbled as he dragged at it with the antler pick he had hurriedly retrieved from the camp. He had seen Rope-in-Hand watching him suspiciously when he went to fetch it, but he no longer cared greatly what she thought. He was being and doing what he was meant to be and to do.

A hare hopped lazily out from a clump of flower-laden thorn bushes. It sat quietly and watched Flint's labours, scratching its neck now and again with a raised hind paw.

'I hope your spirit-brother was not harmed,' Flint said to the hare as he worked. 'He must be safe, I suppose, if he has sent you to me.'

The hare stared mutely back. Flint was glad to have it for an audience. Its presence meant not only that Hare had survived their encounter with the furious spirit of the bees, but also that his curiosity had woken. And curiosity was the only way Flint had yet found to fully engage his guide's interest and support.

'What message should we have you take back to him?' Flint mused. 'Tell him that the essence of these bees is no longer their own. It has been poisoned by the sickness of this tree in which they have made their nest, and that sickness has a human form. It rises from the roots. I think the meaning of that is clear, is it not?'

He glanced over towards the hare. It had not moved, but those dark eyes were no longer upon him. They stared now at a thicket of hazel off beyond Flint, and they did so with rapt and—so Flint thought—hostile attention. He turned his head, in time to see the flicker of movement and hear the breaking of twigs as a second, uninvited observer scurried away through the undergrowth.

Flint grunted in both irritation and relief.

'It's only a Mouse,' he said to the hare. 'An unfriendly one, to be sure, but just a Mouse.'

He dug once more into the loam with his pick, and reached down to scoop out handfuls of it. His fingertips felt something harder than a root, softer than stone. He tugged it free, and smiled. A bone, stained by the earth in which it had lain. A human shin bone.

As HE walked back through the gathering dusk, Flint heard the delicate notes of a flute, riding the warm breeze like petals. He emerged from the woods to find the little camp in its sandy hollow bathed in the day's last soft light. People were readying themselves for the night, going quietly and unhurriedly about their tasks. It filled him with a sudden sense of protective affection.

He had bones pouched inside a bag woven from grass. That shin, and the others that had emerged from the ground after it: a kneecap, some little pieces of finger, a rib. Half a jawbone. He did not know yet quite what they meant, but he knew that they had cast a shadow over this place, and these people, and that only he could lift it.

'What have you got there?'

Rope-in-Hand asked the question as if she meant to be angered by the answer, whatever it was.

'Bees made Long Dusk sick,' Flint said. 'I wanted to know why. In the end, I had to dig to find out.'

'And what did you uncover?'

'Bones.'

She was surprised. He saw it clearly, though she stifled it quickly. Whatever she had expected, it had not been that.

'You can call Long Dusk's illness a matter for the wise women if you wish,' Flint said, 'but death, and the dead—these are matters for shamans. Is it not true?'

The woman stared at him. They looked into one another's eyes. Flint did not know what she saw in him, but in her he saw many hues of sentiment.

'Fifth Moon did not think you were ready,' she said wearily. 'He told me that.'

'So you think to protect the people from my failures by forbidding me to do anything? That cannot last, Rope-in-Hand. There must be a shaman. So we must find out, this day or the next, or the one after, whether Fifth Moon was right.'

She shook her head, but it was a gesture without conviction.

'I will not let what happened to Fifth Moon happen to me,' Flint said.

'Death is a matter for shamans,' she agreed at length.

She walked away with her head hung low. Flint would have expected more fire in her. He was not yet as accomplished as a shaman should be at knowing what currents flowed beneath words and the shapes of faces.

One of the younger women, Born-in-Snow, was kneeling nearby, scraping the last few roasted cockles out from a dying fire. It was almost dark now, and her face was lit orange by the embers. She wore a necklace of polished shells. They caught and returned the light like tiny pearly bowls. She was not one of those to have expressed doubts about Flint's suitability as shaman. Not to his face, at least.

'Blue Feather is sick too, now,' she murmured as Flint walked past. 'She coughs and pales just as Long Dusk did. It is starting in others too, I think. It would be good if you could help them.'

'I will,' Flint told her. Then, remembering the end Fifth Moon's over-confidence had led him to, added: 'I will try.'

FLINT LAY down that night in the lee of a deerskin strung between stakes, on a mat of grass, with the unearthed bones gathered in close to his chest. He watched fireflies dancing in the bushes beyond the camp's edge, and listened to Long Dusk's rough breathing and the sound of the others murmuring, and snoring, and scratching in the darkness all about him while the waves rumbled soothingly along the unseen shore.

And as he sank towards sleep, he whispered to the bones, reciting cycles of words that he had heard Fifth Moon speak only once or twice.

In the dream that came after that, he was sitting on one of a ring of smooth, flat rocks that encircled a small fire. The flames were white. Outside that stone circle, the darkness was absolute. But not empty.

Opposite him, across the trembling flames, something moved in the fringes of the gloom. Something malformed or incomplete, that remained just beyond the light's touch.

'Sit,' Flint suggested. 'Share this fire with me.'

He could not keep his voice entirely free of unease. Dreams were not truly things of the spirit world, but a twisted echo of it. Hare could not find him, or aid him, here.

'I found your bones, friend,' he tried again. 'I would help you, if you will let me.'

'No friend of mine.'

The words oozed from the darkness. They contained much cold malice.

'How can you be sure? Tell me your name, and I will tell you mine.'

Whatever—whoever—it was, growled. Or laughed, perhaps. Flint was not sure.

'You do not know me?' the shadows asked him. It was a man's voice, or something close to it. 'No. You do not. I thought you were him, but you are not. So your shaman is gone now? You have taken his place. Is that it?'

'I am a shaman, yes,' Flint said. His discomfort grew with every breath. The light shed by the white flames seemed to be shrinking in towards the fire, the formless night beyond encroaching.

'He is dead, then,' the dream-thing slurred. 'That is why I have woken. He kept me asleep. Buried.'

'Fifth Moon? Is that who you mean?'

'None came to find me.' Each word dropped like icewater from the tip of an icicle into the pool of faltering light around the fire. 'None sang for me or mourned me. There was no sorrow, no rituals for me, no ochre path opened to show me the way onwards. No punishment for him.'

'Who? Fifth Moon?' Flint said again, getting unsteadily to his feet, pushed up by fear.

'I cannot kill the one who killed me. But I can kill you. All of you, who forgot me. One by one.'

The pallid flames snapped out of existence. The blackness boiled in, rushing to fill the space where light had been. It came with a shriek of rage and a gust of contempt towards Flint. Who fled, with all the speed his mind could command, towards wakefulness.

FLINT GROUND red ochre into a flaky powder on the flat stone Fifth Moon had always used for the same purpose. Several of the children stood in fascinated silence, watching attentively. When he was done, he carefully brushed the ochre onto a piece of thin hide, which he folded, pinned with a sliver of bone, and tucked inside his tunic.

He rose a little stiffly to his feet, leaning on his spear. He was tired, for he had not slept after his dream of darkness and anger. The sun was hot again today, but his arms and legs ached with some memory of the cold and the fear that had afflicted him in that place. He could hear now, rising from the amongst the little shelters and the hearths and the soft earth itself, what no one else could: the endless, forbidding, corrupted song of the bees.

He put the sound of the surf at his back and headed for the woods. The young girl Dew-on-Grass was the only one of the children to follow him, trying to put her own feet where his had been.

Some of the adults paused too, watching him go, their silence more apprehensive than that of the children. Rope-in-Hand stood apart from the others, amongst the bushes behind the camp. She looked feverish.

Flint shook the bones in their grass sack.

'Is this who I think it is?' he asked her. 'Did you know what Fifth Moon did to him?'

Rope-in-Hand looked away, casting her gaze out along the line of the beach, following its straight course off into the sun-soaked distance. She clasped her hands together as if hoping they might steady one another.

'No,' she said quietly.

Flint heard the truth in her voice, and heard—because he listened with a shaman's ears—much else besides.

'No,' he said, 'but you wondered.'

She gave a little shrug of her shoulders, still not looking at him. So small and fragile she seemed to him now.

'A people must have a shaman,' she murmured. 'As you said. They must believe in the shaman. I do not want to know what happened. Whatever was done—it could not be undone then, and cannot now. Sometimes silence does less harm than questions asked, answers given.'

'I only want to make Long Dusk and Blue Feather and the rest well again,' Flint said. 'If I do not do this, they will be dead before we leave for the acorn groves. Maybe all of us will be.'

Rope-in-Hand said nothing. Beneath her silence, Flint listened to the thrumming, insistent drone in which the sickness dwelled. It would never leave, he knew, unless he sent it away.

'You are burdened,' he said, understanding and certainty coming even as he spoke, so entwined with the words that he could not tell which followed the other. 'By loss, by your silent doubts. By your wish to keep our people safe; safe from secrets, from shamans who are not ready. I can take some of these burdens from you, and share those that remain.'

At last she turned her face to him, and amidst all the other things that shaped it, he saw something new there. Hope, perhaps.

'Tell me his name,' Flint said. 'I was very young. I do not remember his name, or never knew it. Tell me the name of the man Fifth Moon killed to lie next to you.'

'Crow,' Rope-in-Hand said. 'His name was Crow.'

Flint left her and walked into the shade of the trees.

'Let him go, child,' he heard her saying to Dew-on-Grass behind him. 'He wants to be a shaman, so let him go and be one. You wait here, where it is safe. We will see. We will see whether he comes back or not.'

FLINT LAID the bones out under the oak tree. He put them on the ground beneath which the rest of Crow's body still lay. Above, the hive was silent and still. As if, he thought, what lay within was waiting for him.

He opened out the folded hide and spat onto the red ochre it contained. He rubbed it into a paste with his thumb, then spread it over the bones. As he did all this, he sang to himself, and to the bones and through them to the spirit he must find, and hold and send on its way.

Flint crossed his legs and straightened his back. He laid the dyed bones in his lap and rested one hand upon them. With his other hand, he tapped out a soft call to Hare on his finger drum. Slowly, slightly, he rocked backwards and forwards. He closed his eyes. Allowed himself to die a little. And journeyed.

Hare met him by the greater, stronger tree in the deep world.

'Thank you for saving me from the bees,' said Flint.

Hare loped a little closer.

'It was instinct,' he said casually. 'I couldn't help myself.'

'Thank you, even so.'

'What are we doing now?' Hare asked, sitting back on his haunches.

'We have to call up the bees again, and I will free them of the spirit that has taken hold of them. I will send it along the ochre path, to the Sunset Lands, where it can rest. It cannot harm my people from there.'

Hare stared at him. Only a tremor in his tall ears betrayed the guide's discomfiture.

'Bravery and foolishness often piss in the same river,' Hare observed.

'What does that mean?'

'Just that. Bravery and foolishness often—,'

'Never mind. I will need your help, if you are willing.'

'You brought your spear, I see,' Hare observed.

Flint looked at his own hand. In its red grasp—bright red, since the ochre shone with its power here—it clasped his stone-tipped spear. He had imagined himself coming armed into the spirit world this time.

'It seemed wise,' he murmured.

'Wisdom's a good thing in a shaman,' Hare said. 'Fear is useful too, I always thought. Keeps carelessness at bay. Keeps both a shaman and his guide safe.'

Flint smiled.

'I brought my fear with me too.'

'Good. Mine is also in close attendance. Let's begin, then.'

THE BEES came forth as soon as Hare whispered into the tree. This time, as they swarmed amongst the uppermost branches like a storm of pebbles, Flint was ready for the shock and for the weight of their anger. He steadied himself.

Hare sprang down from amongst the high branches and stood at Flint's side.

'Come down, little brothers, and speak with us,' Hare called in a singing voice, and whispered to Flint from the corner of his mouth: 'It's still not speaking they mean to do, though.'

The cloud of bees plummeted, a dark shaft of noise that struck the ground hard enough to stagger Flint, and then surged up once more into the roiling form of a man. Flint tightened his grip upon his spear, and spoke before the tormented spirit had time to rush upon him.

'There is no need to hide,' Flint he said, thumping the butt of his spear on the ground. He was surprised at the firmness of his own voice. He hoped that might last a little while longer, at least. 'I have painted your bones. I have opened a path for you.'

Fluttering waves ran through the swarm-shape, as thousands upon thousands of winged bodies shifted and moved against one another. When they ceased, what stood before Flint was no longer the imagined form of a man, but the man himself, wearing a skin of living bees.

'I will not go,' the man said, and his voice was the hum of wings, the rustle of uncountable legs. 'I am not finished.'

'Yes, you are finished. I cannot undo the wrongs you suffered, but I cannot let you stay either.'

'Fifth Moon was stronger than you. He killed me. He had power over me, so long as he lived. You do not.'

'But I do. I have your name, Crow, and your painted bones, and I have the need of a shaman to preserve the people he serves.'

'What does he mean, Fifth Moon killed him?' said Hare in indignant surprise. 'I don't know anything about that. It can't be right.'

'Hush,' said Flint.

He extended his free arm sideways, pointing into the world of shifting lights and mists and shapes. He formed an image in his mind, and believed in it with all his heart, and the spirit world conformed to his belief. A red path laid itself out. An ochre path.

'I have opened the way for you,' he said, as he had before, but this time he made it a command, and a promise. 'No path was offered you before. The one who came before me made your death a secret, and a lie, to serve his own hungers. I am sorry for that. Now it is time to travel to the Sunset Lands, and rest.'

A few bees fell from Crow's brow, spinning dizzily down. Flint saw skin, dark with earth. The dead man looked along the ochre path stretching away from them. More fragments of his living carapace broke off and now Flint could see an eye, and the edge of a terrible wound that had broken in the side of Crow's face.

'It was unjust,' moaned Crow. 'To be killed by a shaman, my own shaman, for want of a woman—.' His voice tailed off as bees spilled from him.

'A woman?' murmured Hare disbelievingly, but Flint quieted him with a wave of his hand.

'It was unjust,' he said to Crow, 'but shamans are only men, as weak and flawed as any other. Our sight can become clouded, just as yours has.' In saying it, Flint knew it to be true in a way he had not before, and in knowing it he both condemned and forgave Fifth Moon. And Crow. 'I cannot let you punish those who do not deserve it.'

Crow looked at him. His face was almost wholly exposed, and the swarm had loosened itself from about his shoulders and his arms. Flint felt a blossom of confidence in his breast, knowing for the first time that he would succeed in this.

And then his legs were burning, tingling slabs of pain. He looked down at them in bewilderment and saw nothing amiss, yet stinging pulses beat in them. His concentration wavered.

'What are you doing?' hissed Hare in alarm.

Crow's eyes narrowed. A shadow that had seemed to be lifting from them fell across them once more.

'Shaman,' Hare muttered urgently.

The bees were rising again, closing themselves over Crow's face. Flint's thighs and groin were alive with itching points of pain. He could feel his spirit being tugged back towards his body, and see the deep world dimming about him.

'Shaman!' Hare yelped.

But Flint was blinking blearily, seeing grass, and patches of blue sky, and trees all about. He could feel the burden of his body once more. He was alive. He looked down into his lap, and found a writhing mat of ants and dried leaves and twigs. He was too amazed, and too numbed by his wrenching return from the other world, to do more than sit, staring at the dark mass and feeling the fire of their bites burning in his skin.

His muscles acted where his mind could not, and flung him to his feet. Crow's ochre-red bones fell to the ground. Flint slapped and scraped at his leggings and his stomach, knocking showers of ants free. He hopped and jumped and shook himself, trying to dislodge the most tenacious of his tiny assailants from within and under his clothes.

There was an abandoned bowl of woven rushes lying beside him, still holding the portion of the anthill that had not been emptied into his lap. Shrill laughter was coming from the nearest bushes.

'Mouse!' shouted Flint, choked for a moment by an anger such as he had never known.

He heard the boy running off, and had to crush the instinct to give chase. Instead, he staggered a few paces to find a patch of ground clear of scurrying ants and slumped back down. His heart was thudding in his chest, his skin still fiery, but he closed his eyes and reached, reached.

There was no time for the proper preparations, no time to ready himself. By force of will he tore his spirit free from its fleshly frame, knowing that such violence might make it difficult to return.

He fell, and tumbled, and was buffeted by the jarring crossing from one world to another. When he stood once again in the land of the spirits, his vision was marred by dark veins of shadow bleeding in from the edges. His hearing was blurred, as if his head had been sunk into a pool. He could see and hear just enough, though.

Hare was trying to take flight, bucking and struggling, but bees and Crow, merged once more, had hold of one his hind legs and were hauling him back towards the tree. The great vein of decay in the tree's trunk had split and now stood open like a hungry, waiting maw.

Flint looked to his side. The ochre path still lay where he had cast it. That at least he had done right. He set both hands upon his spear and ran at Crow. The dead man's damaged spirit remained unaware of Flint's return, until the very moment that the shaman's spear transfixed it.

Bees erupted in every direction, a great expanding fog of them that engulfed Flint. Crow twisted and turned, bending the spear's shaft with the vigour of his struggles. Flint shuffled sideways, fearful that he lacked the strength this moment required. Crow turned his head, saw Flint, and growled. A plume of bees gushed from his mouth and lashed at Flint, who felt the blows like a rain of sharp stones lacerating him, flaying away the layers of his soul. Still he heaved at the spear, and at last Crow's foot touched ochre.

'Go,' Flint cried. 'I have opened the way for you.'

He flung himself, and the spear, and Crow, forward onto the path that pointed the way to the Sunset Lands. A piercing howl drowned out all thought. An ochreous tint suffused everything, as if a red sun had risen. Flint could no longer feel the spear in his hands. For a timeless span, he was formless and faint and dwindling.

Then Hare had his teeth about Flint's wrist, and was pulling at him, dragging him on his back out of the path's powerful flow. Flint sat up and the two of them, shaman and guide, watched as the last vestiges of red faded. The ochre path was gone, and Crow was gone.

Flint could not rise to his feet. He sat there, feeble as the smallest child, watching the confused bees rushing in helpless circles.

'It will take them some time to remember themselves,' Hare said.

'You should help them,' Flint suggested.

'If you like.' Hare rolled his head from side to side, his ears rocking back and forth. 'That wasn't how Fifth Moon would have done it.'

'I think I will not be doing anything the way Fifth Moon would have done it,' said Flint.

Hare sniffed. 'No. I suppose not. You'll have to tell me, some time, how this happened. I can't believe Fifth Moon would have—.'

'Some time,' agreed Flint. 'Not now. I cannot stay.'

His weariness was terrible, and his memories of the world of the living were distant, fragile things that felt as if they might slip away from him all together if he did not reclaim them now.

'Will you do something for me?' he asked Hare.

'Of course, shaman.' There was no hint of mockery in the words.

'There is a favour I would have you ask of the bees, on my behalf. Once they have calmed a little.'

FLINT SLEPT though the rise and fall of both moon and sun. He slept dreamlessly, for which he was grateful afterwards. When he woke, his body felt sluggish, as if it had forgotten how to contain him. But he was alive, and that was, he knew, as much as he could have asked for.

Long Dusk sat by a fire, baking fish wrapped in leaves. She coughed, and her face was gaunt, but she smiled at Flint as he passed. There was no sickness here now. There was no malign drone in the background, only the raucous cries of gulls wheeling high above. Flint walked through a camp content with itself, and with the bounteous season. Born-in-Snow offered him water, freshly carried from the nearby stream. He savoured its coolness in his throat. Fathead grinned foolishly at the sight of the shaman, and slapped his thigh in delight.

He saw Rope-in-Hand, kneeling to scrape at a deerskin pegged out over a flat stone. She paused and looked up. She nodded to him, just once. It was enough. It was the making of a grateful bargain. A sharing of burdens, and silence. And leadership.

Flint went up onto the bank and stretched himself out on the ground. The sun's warmth was in the air and in the earth beneath him. It was in the breeze that stirred the grasses and made them dance at the edges of his vision. He wanted to gather as much of it as he could into himself.

'Did you make Long Dusk better, then?'

Flint had to wince against the glare to make out Dew-on-Grass' silhouette.

'That is what they are saying,' she told him.

Before he could answer, a succession of high-pitched yelps rang out. There was some small commotion in the camp.

'What is happening?' asked Flint lazily.

Dew-on-Grass paused for a moment, then grunted.

'It looks like Mouse. Running around.'

Another sharp, childish cry of protest.

'I think there are bees chasing him,' Dew-on-Grass said in a mildly surprised tone of voice.

'Oh,' said Flint.

'Is it true you saved us, then?' Dew-on-Grass asked, Mouse and his unfortunate plight already forgotten. 'Are you a great shaman now?'

'Not great, no. Just a shaman. Full of flaws.'

Flint smiled and closed his eyes, surrendering himself to the sun's cosseting embrace.

The Death of a Love

HAL DUNCAN

1

ntros for stories always seem strange to me. When Pat invited me to contribute to this anthology, given the good cause it was in, I was glad to have this story, just finished, ready to be sent off then and there. A chance to turn my impractical scribbling skills to the service of something real, to earn some money for a breast cancer charity? Damn straight, man.

Of course, then he had to go and ask me for an intro.

Thing is, I'm one of those minimal cover letter guys who reckons all you tell upfront is the title and the word count. What if I choose the wrong way to pitch it to you? What if I sketch in "what it's about", and that narrows your focus, like it's only about that? Really, I'd rather you just came to it cold.

Besides, other writers get all the cool intros. They always seem to have stories behind their stories. The year they spent herding lemurs on a kibbutz in Israel. The kid next door with a badger for a hand. Being on acid in CBGB's back in '76. And so on. With me, it's more like: um… I had an idea? Don't ask me when I had it; I usually can't remember. Don't ask me where it came from; I'm fucked if I know. I was probably having a cup of tea and a cigarette at the time.

But sometimes a story does have roots. It's probably not coincidence that a story called "The Death of a Love" came along after a painful-but-inevitable break-up salved with episodes of The Wire watched back-to-back through the empty nights. It's probably not happenstance that I had the notion, while downing a box of red wine and listening to "Love on the Rocks" on repeat, that a writer can be like a homicide cop of the heart — investigating, interrogating, a keen eye on the subtext of every situation. If you want to write stories that are relevant, it's kind of your job to walk the mean streets of the city of soul, to try and solve those sorry cases of the human condition, the hidden whys and hows of relationships. Which doesn't always make you the most well-adjusted individual when it comes to your own.

True love? Yeah, I know that story, kid. He said, pouring another glass.

But see, now I've said too much, because that's not "what it's about", not in the end. If the narrator is cynical, I'm kind of cynical about his cynicism, to be honest. Alcohol and maudlin music? Yeah, I know that story too.

So I'm going to shut up now, and let you read the damn story. What's it about? It's about 6000 words. Where did the idea come from? Well, the address is on the cover letter.

❖

*T*he death of a love is a hard thing to take. Most loves die of natural causes, of course, just fade away slowly over days or weeks, months or years, until there's just a scrap of a ghost, echoes of the good times and the salad days, haunting a home like the tobacco-stink of last night's party, or trailing after two ex-lovebirds as they go their separate ways, clinging to their clothes like each other's perfume or cologne, whispering in their ear when they listen to a certain song. Most loves just have their natural lifespan and after that they weaken and they die. That's the way of things. But it's hard to take, so it's weird but maybe not surprising how a lot of times you see those 'birds stay together after their love is dead, after all that's left is a shadow.

You look for that fat little pink-skinned cupid with its white wings, but it just ain't there. The little fucker is dead and gone.

I mean, sometimes it's not what it seems. Some of those ghost loves, you find they're not really dead at all, so much as…dissolved into every little thing that makes up a life together. You're interviewing the parents of a suspect, say. Sitting in some floral-patterned armchair, right? Watching them sit there on the sofa across from you. They don't hold each other's hands. They don't even sit that close to each other. Hell, maybe the wife will be sat down on the sofa while the husband's over at the drinks cabinet, pouring himself a malt whisky. You look around the room, and you see the photographs and the knick-knacks, everything perfectly in place, and it just seems so fucking hollow. You think: this couple, their love died years ago; there's no passion here, no deep desire, just fucking habit. Once upon a time they might have had a cupid fluttering back and forth between them, lighting on her lap now and then, or his shoulder. But that love's flown the coop long ago. That's what you think.

But then…then you notice the wife's gaze drifting across to the photo of the kids. Or maybe the husband will walk across the room and rest his hand on her shoulder. Or something, you know, something like that? And you feel this…presence in the house.

You can smell it—roses and chocolate and popcorn, maybe, or some other set of smells, sweet and soft or rich, ripe even. You catch a glimpse out of the corner of your eye, a flutter of feathers or a flash of flame, a reflection in a mirror or the glass of a picture frame. Or you hear it—echoes of laughter maybe, a faint hint of a fairground tune. That's when you realize that their love isn't really dead at all; the little bastard's just gone quiet, hid itself in every corner of their life. It's kind of sweet, when you think about it. Like it's become a secret between these two, their silent invisible love. They're still 'birds, you know? They just sing quietly, just for each other.

That's what my folks were like, you know? Before the old man died. I didn't realize it till after, always thought their love was long-dead of neglect, what with the old man hardly ever home, always working nights on this case or that, and closed in on himself whenever he *was* in the house, drinking to forget those cases. It was only after his death that their love sorta…came out of the woodwork, I guess you could say, when my mother needed it most. Fuck me, if I don't go round to visit one day and hear her in the kitchen, chatting away to some chirping canary or some such, I think; only when I walk in, turns out it's their fucking love, this cute little bastard of a cupid, flying round her as she washes dishes, chattering away in this language of whistles and chirps that only she and it understand. Where the fuck was *that* hiding all these years? I thought. Where the fuck was that when I was laying in bed at night, listening to them argue about how the force was killing him.

But, you know, after a while, watching the cupid perch on the refrigerator that he'd grab a beer from, or the kitchen chair that used to be his, or the counter-top where he'd lay his badge down, I understood it was *always* there; I was just too dumb to notice it as a kid. And if there's only two of them speak that weird birdsong language now, it used to be three.

It's a different story for a lot of 'birds, like when the love turns to stone—that I've seen as well. I mean, you can be in the exact same house, with the exact same floral-patterned armchair, exact same sofa, exact same fucking *scatter cushions*, and I tell you, if you don't catch at least a hint of something still going on between the husband and wife—you take a close look at what's around you. Ten to one what you'll see, up on the mantelpiece or on some fucking dresser in the bedroom, is that little butt-naked cupid frozen forever like some plaster cherub. You might even think it looks cute at first, but look closer, at the face. Sometimes they're blank, but a lot of time they're sad. Sometimes they're fucking screaming. Like Han fucking Solo in carbonite.

Swear to God, that type always have their dead love on display somewhere, like a fucking statue. I don't understand those fucks, really I don't. You let your love go cold and still, let it turn to stone, and you put it up on a shelf like a fucking trophy. What's that about? You want to have your grandmother's ashes up on a shelf, that's one thing. You want to send Old Yeller to the taxidermist because you can't stand him being gone—fine. But your dead love...

Shit, one time—the Armitage case—I was interviewing this yuppie couple—mid-thirties at the oldest, in-laws of the suspects—and they had their love sat up in a glass-fronted cabinet, in this Chesterfield kinda thing, right between a model of the Eiffel Tower and a fucking snowglobe of Lady Liberty. The husband, he catches me looking at it, and you know what he says? *It's beautiful, right?* What kind of fucked-up shit is that, I ask you? Fuck, I know you can't always blame the 'birds for their love going south—shit happens—but these fucks, they don't even question that maybe it's their own fucking neglect killed what they had; they don't even get what they've lost, I realize. To them everything is A-OK and they're proud of it. Never mind the Sixties, I remember thinking, these fuckers have barely caught up with emancipation; to them that love is still something that *belongs* to them, a fucking piece of property, not a living, breathing, laughing, crying *being*. Or the stone-cold mortal remains of one. That kind of attitude to their children and we'd be calling Social Services on the bastards.

That was damn near my first case, actually. I was such a fucking rookie. I remember mouthing off to my partner afterward, Jackman, in The Lizard Lounge, elbow on the bar, waving my beer as I fucking testified: *How can they be like that? What the fuck kind of robotic assholes are these people?* Fuck, I was a real hothead about it; I was so sure that kind of creepy shit put the finger on them, that these heartless freaks had to be the perps, *had* to be. I don't know. Maybe a little of it was I still thought my folks were that way, an empty shell of a relationship with a dead love inside; I didn't see what they really had going between them, so I hated the old man for a while because I thought he'd let their love die. And maybe that's what made me follow him onto the force as much as anything, made me push for this department. I wanted to sort that kind of shit out. I was a self-righteous little bastard.

Cause all that's just the fucking cherry on the icing—the shadow loves and the stone loves, the cupids dead from lack of due care. What you bite down on in my line of work, every single fucking day of the week, is the big-ass hunk of cake made of chocolate-colored bullshit, bitter lemons and sour grapes. Cause most loves die of natural causes, sure, and even neglect is natural at the end of the day. You gotta let that love live for itself, find its own way, even if that freedom is the freedom to fade away or go cold; a cupid's progenitors don't *own* it, you know? So you gotta let it be what it's gonna be, live and die by its own will.

But those that don't die natural…ah, shit…it makes me sick to my fucking stomach sometimes.

You talk to Homicide, Narcotics, Vice, they'll all tell you that they deal with the worst of it—the psychopaths, the drug-dealers, the kiddie porn peddlers; but they ain't got nothing on Erocide. *You* stand on the wharf, I tell them, you stand on the fucking wharf as they pull a three-day old floater out of the water, some poor fucking cupid with its wings all ragged and torn, half the feathers missing and what's left filthy with oil and shit, used condoms and fuck knows what all caught up in them. You look at that baby-soft pink skin all purple and blotchy now, I say, half-eaten by the fishes. You take a good fucking look at that bloated belly and the tongue so fat it spills out of the mouth, like a sick fucking caricature of the podgy little imp it used to be. You look at the fucking strangle marks round its neck, and you tell me that's not a million times worse than any of the shit *you* have to deal with. That's some couple's love, their fucking heart and soul, their hopes and dreams, murdered and dumped like a stray dog. That's a dead child, a crack baby and an abuse victim all rolled into one. That's the worst there is.

And nine times out of ten, it was one of the victim's own 'birds that done it. Shit, *more* than nine times out of ten.

Sure, every so often, every once in a while, you find it's some vicious bastard with an axe to grind, a family-member or so-called friend, some twisted little fuck who can't stand for your two 'birds to have what they don't. Believe me, I've seen them all: the father who don't think his would-be son-in-law is high class enough; the mother who can't let her baby boy love anyone but mommy dearest; the stalker who's sure their cupid is just hiding until this upstart is out of the picture; the angry ex-boyfriend who knows, who *knows* that him and his girl never really had shit together, just a flap of white feathers overhead when they were fucking, but still he blames it all on this bitch who broke his heart. Sure, you get those bastards, the ones who hide their bitterness, stay close to the 'birds and do their damnedest to destroy the love they hate, smiling all the time.

That's what I thought we had with the Armitage case, with the in-laws—that yuppie couple with their dead love in the fucking souvenir cabinet. They had to be all fucked-up on the inside, I thought, even if it didn't show; she had to be jealous of her brother and his new wife, what they had together; he had to feel like less of a man than Armitage, not being able to keep his love alive. I couldn't shake that image of the stone cupid in the cabinet, couldn't see how anyone could be that twisted. *Fuck, Jackman, I remember saying, would you pickle a fucking cot death and put the jar up on display?*

Don't remember Jackman saying anything to that, just raising his glass to his lips, taking a sip of whisky.

I'd learn.

Those types of love-killings are rarer than you'd think, I'd learn, swear to God. A love can be a tough little bastard when it comes to outside influences set on breaking it up. Disapproving parents might drive your Romeo and Juliet to their deaths, but likely as not they'll just drive them out of town, and those 'birds will fly off into the wilds with a passion that's stronger than if the dumb-ass parents hadn't tried to split them up in the first place. The stalkers and the jilted, they can try to poison the love they hate with lies and rumors, but most likely it'll just come back and bite them on the ass—literally—a bona fide pint-sized angel of vengeance with teeth and fingernails sharp as a cat's claws.

Fuck, most pathetic thing I ever saw was an attempted erocide by an old harpy whose sister met the man of her dreams one day. These two spinsters are both in their seventies, been living together all their lives—fucking Patti and Selma we called them—then suddenly, bam! Selma's got a cupid fluttering round her every time she sees this guy she met down at the bingo, every time she talks about him; and this cupid is getting more and more solid with every date. Patti, she sees herself ending up alone, and she can't stand it. But she doesn't let on. No, she plays it like this is the best thing ever, makes like she adores the little sprite, she's so fucking happy for her sister. She's making nice with it, cooing and petting it all the time. Of course, turns out every night she's creeping out of bed, sneaking into her sister's room, and trying to smother it with a pillow while it's sleeping at the foot of her bed. What makes it so pathetic is the more she does this, the stronger it gets. See, somehow, somewhere in her heart, Selma can tell that there's something not right here. All Patti's fussing, it starts to seem kinda creepy, just a little too intense, so slowly but surely Selma starts to back off from her sister. She starts talking about it to her fella, of course; hell, it just brings her and him even closer together. Anyway, it all comes to a head one night when Selma wakes up to find Patti fucking *gone*. In the head, I mean. She's lost it, totally bat-shit fucking crazy, all her old maid weight on top of the pillow as she tries to suffocate the cupid, screaming at it over and over: *just die already, just die, just die!*

Almost felt sorry for her, when we carted her away. That cupid looked as bright-eyed as a prom queen's first crush.

Point is, more often than not, that sort of shit just backfires completely. You put a bullet in someone's love and if they know it was you…well, that love might spend a night in intensive care but it'll be all the better for it in the morning. Unless you can persuade your victims that one or both of them is to blame...hell, I've seen loves rise from the deathbed like Lazarus, fucking fireworks lighting up the sky, soon as both 'birds found out it was all a mistake. No, he didn't really cheat on her. No, she never said that about him. It was just some scheming little shit trying to wreck their relationship, and not the almighty mindfuck by their partner they'd been led to think it was. Boom! Fwoosh! Fucking happy ever afters like a fucking Disney movie.

Just not that many of them.

See, that's not the usual story. Nine times out of ten—*more* than nine times out of ten—it *is* one or both of the 'birds to blame. Because people are fucking dumb, and they're fucking greedy. They're blind, and they're selfish, and they're just plain fucking crazy. I learned that with the Armitages. There I am, this fucking rookie, railing on at Jackman about how it had to be the creepy in-laws. My second or third case, it was, I think. Jackman, he just shakes his head. *You didn't watch the 'birds,* he says. *I told you to watch the 'birds.*

That's what he'd said to me when I asked why it was us going to notify the victim's progenitors, why they didn't just send two uniforms? And what the fuck were we going to say anyway? Shit, how do you tell a couple of bright young lovebirds that their cupid is down at the city morgue after being pulled out of a dumpster? How do you tell them that its face is pulped so bad they may not recognize it, skull caved in to a different shape, compound fractures to its forearms where it tried to stave off the assault, wings hacked off and as yet unlocated—dumped separately, we were reckoning, in the hope that the body might be misidentified as a human child's? Like you could ever mistake the scent of a cupid, no matter how fucking rank the smell of petrol and burnt flesh coating it. Like you could really mask that beautiful aroma of coffee and home cooking, of rosewater and bergamot, of a thousand other things you just know mean something wonderful to someone. To *two* someones, rather.

You let me do the talking, Jackman had said. *You just listen and watch the 'birds.*

But I didn't listen, and I didn't watch them, not properly. All I saw was two progenitors devastated by the news of the death of their love. All I heard was the hollow echoes of broken dreams recited in broken voices. How they'd been childhood sweethearts. How they'd been living together for two years now, engaged for one. How they had their wedding just there in June. All the things people say mechanically as they realize they don't mean shit anymore. I took some of it in; I noticed the way she cried and he just looked at her helplessly, the way she didn't even turn to him for comfort, the way that even when he moved in to hug her there was a distance, an awkwardness between them. Like they were going through the motions. But their love was dead, right? That thing they'd had between them, that fusion of souls that had once made them reach out to each other without thinking, in times of need, to console or be consoled—that was gone, battered to death by some sick fuck with a tire iron, a crowbar, fuck knows what. How the fuck you expect a couple to be there for each other after that?

That's another thing makes erocide the fucking worst. Can you imagine what it's like to lose a child, but for the one person you share that grief with to be taken away and replaced by a stranger you don't know at all, a complete stranger sitting across the breakfast table from you, looking into your eyes and feeling nothing, just as you look at them and feel nothing? Can you imagine what that's like? I don't know that I can. I don't know that I want to.

They said they'd sort of known—the Armitages, I mean—said they'd felt something was wrong when they got back from the movies and their love wasn't around; but they but didn't really admit it to themselves. They'd gone to bed tired, feeling weird, disconnected, but it wasn't until they got up the next morning that the absence really dug its nails into them. That was when they'd phoned in the missing person's report. Cupids go AWOL all the time, play hide-and-seek with you, wander off on a whim, disappear into the shadows only to leap out when you least expect it. They're fucking *capricious*, right? But the Armitages, they said they'd felt that this was different. They'd known.

I remember Jackman nodded at that.

But me, I didn't pay attention. I didn't listen and watch. So when we start interviewing the friends and family, when we meet the in-laws with their stone cupid in a cabinet, I think we've got the killer or killers in front of us. The two couples are close, have keys to each other's apartments. This pair are fucking freaks and they're getting their noses rubbed in it by the newlyweds. Who are away at the movies leaving their little cupid home alone. That's means, motive and opportunity, right? And, come on, who the fuck is going to off their own love then call in a missing person's and draw attention to it? When you could just lay low for a month or two then tell everyone your love just faded away? That was my genius logic.

Sometimes people are dumb or greedy, Jackman said to me. This was in the Lizard Lounge after I'd been laying down How I Saw It. *Sometimes they're blind or selfish or just fucking crazy. But sometimes afterwards they're smart enough to know that if a dead cupid gets traced back to its progenitors that whole story's going to fall apart.*

He was right, of course, more right than I knew. I've been working Erocide now for about as many years as he had been then, and in those years now I've seen all sorts of fucked-up shit from perps trying to make cupid corpses unidentifiable: burning off fingerprints with acid so you can't match them to the 'birds; gouging out eyes so you can't do retina scans for the progenitor's images, cutting out their double-hearts and scattering the bits so you can't piece together IDs from the shared memories. At the end of the day though, a couple's love is built so much out of the two of them that their fucking names are coded in its bones. Some solid forensics and some god old-fashioned footwork…sooner or later you're most likely going to find your way to the right door. Doesn't mean we can tie a love-killer to the crime, of course, but if they've been telling all their friends about the slow wasting of their late love to a frail wraith…and we've got an all-too solid skeleton… well, then they have some explaining to do. Sometimes the perps do have the sense not to dig too deep a hole for themselves like that. A lot of the time. Shit, if there's no missing person's report matching your body, and the perp has done their best to make it difficult to identify, most likely what you have is a cover-up, where the love you're dealing with was as hidden in life as it was in death. A love that was fucked from the beginning.

I don't know what the worst case I've dealt with was, but it's a good bet that it was a cover-up. I mean, mostly they're just run-of-the-mill…snuffed-out affairs, aborted flings. Some Joe Schmoe has a mid-life crisis and sparks up an affair with his wife's best friend, you know? He's been with his wife for ten, fifteen years though, so when their love starts to fade suddenly he gets cold feet. He doesn't know what he wants. He wants the best of both worlds. He's confused, torn. Guilt makes him compensate, try to rebuild the love he has with his wife. But all the while he's trying to hide this other little cupid, too greedy to give it up but trying *really* fucking hard not to let it show, not to think of the best friend, of the times when they're together, of the thrill of it all. You ever tried *really* fucking hard not to think of someone?

It's a surefire way of getting them stuck in your mind like a bad jingle. So slowly but surely Joe drives himself crazy. One day he just loses it while he's with the best friend. *I can't do this anymore*, he says. *This is fucked-up. I love my wife.* Then they get into an argument—maybe it's just the first of many—and sooner or later he's pacing this way and that, shouting all sorts of bullshit at her. They start blaming each other for everything under the sun, cause the guilt is eating away at them both. They're screaming in each other's faces. Finally…finally he grabs that cupid by the throat and he strangles the life out of it right in front of her.

Those are the ones we fish out of the river, or dig out of a shallow grave, with their eyes gouged out and their fingerprints burned off. The perp, he panics, but then he gets to thinking, nobody knows about this, just the two of us. Nobody else needs to *ever* know about it. And sometimes, I'm sure, nobody else ever does.

I think my first ever case was a drowned cupid that never did get IDed. Fingers cut off with secateurs or some such, eyes gone, heart never found. The bones gave up names alright, but they were all pet-names—Sweety, Honey, Kitten, Pumpkin, Baby. Forensics said there might be a John or a Joan or a Jean or a Jan in there, but that was the best they could do. *Love,* I remember Jackman saying, *doesn't generally give a fuck what's on the driver's license.*

Sometimes, the cover-ups are as easy to trace as the Armitages, the names shining out of the bones for all to see. Sometimes not.

Those are just the common-or-garden cover-ups though, the one-offs; there's much worse than that. You get a serial philanderer with the right fucked-up mindset and you can end up with a backwoods cemetery of shallow graves filled with murdered loves. One guy we brought in, turned out he had a hundred and forty-three fucking bodies in bits under the floorboards of his apartment.

He wasn't married; it wasn't that he was trying to hide anything. Psyche evaluation said he wasn't even a psychopath by the normal tests; he just "couldn't face commitment." So he'd get himself into one relationship after another and he'd destroy them, one after another. Soon as each cupid appeared he'd grab it, chain it up in his closet. *Chain* it up. He needed the love, you know, so he'd let the relationship grow, but he couldn't fucking handle it like a fucking human being so he'd keep that love hidden from the women. The women, they didn't understand what the fuck was going on. It felt like love but there was no fucking cupid. And then eventually, with each of them, he'd reach a point where it was all just too fucking serious, so he'd kill the little bastard. Next time the woman comes round, there's nothing between them; it's like there never *was* anything between them. And she walks away, wondering how she ever fooled herself into thinking they had something. A hundred and forty-three bodies. It was a fucking slaughterhouse that smelled of hot dogs in the park and vanilla incense.

It was the closet case cover-ups Jackman hated the most, and I can't say as I blame him. You could usually tell them right off, because a couple's love always looks sorta like a mix of the two 'birds—one eye of his colour, the other of hers, his fingerprints on one hand, hers on the other, and so on—and that goes all the way down to most cupids being hermaphrodites. Most, I say. If you find a cupid that's wholly male, you can be pretty sure you have a closet case on your hand. You know at least that its progenitors were two gay guys, and if it's a cover-up…well, when someone's hacked away at the genitalia in some botch-job attempt to disguise what's going on down there, it's not hard to put two and two together and work out why that love ended up dead. You trace that shit back and half the time you find two frightened fifteen year olds who just panicked before anyone could tell them nobody really gives a shit these days. Don't get me wrong; it's still an erocide and Jackman and me, we'd work the case just like any other. It's just that it brings the bullshit of it all right home to you. Like the Sanchez/Rodriguez case—two kids from the projects, running with the gangs and hard as nails, but scared shitless their compadres would discover they had a thing for each other. So they dealt with their problem the simplest way they knew, emptied the clips of their automatics into it. Thing is, it wasn't that they were horrified at wanting to do the down and dirty with each other; they didn't give a fuck for any idea of what's sinful and sordid; they just bought into a game, and having power in that game meant sacrificing soul for status. They still fucked every day, they told us in the interview room; they just took down the billboard that advertised the fact. That's what Jackman hated about it, not the poor little repressed gayboy bullshit, but the fact that it was so fucking senseless.

Dumb or greedy. Blind or selfish. Or just plain crazy.

Sometimes seems like it's all of the above.

I don't know if it's the worst, but the cover-up case that got under my skin the most was the Henderson cupid, a body that was little more than a bag of broken bones, found in an abandoned subway tunnel. It was Forensics' finest hour, that case, but it still gives me the creeps. All the flesh had been stripped from the skeleton, and a hammer and a hacksaw taken to it; this cupid had been taken apart into a fucking human jigsaw puzzle. That's not the bad part though. The reason this cupid had been taken apart so thoroughly became obvious as the reconstruction job went on and the skeleton began to take shape—or misshape, rather. You get disabled cupids, of course; there's no reason that you wouldn't. They all look pretty much like your plain old-fashioned cherub, but then so do babies; and they all inherit a fair amount of their physical features from their progenitors, just like babies. Now I ain't exactly a paid-up member of the PC Brigade, but that sort of shit never meant anything to me. Some people, they still think in terms of Romantic bullshit, like a beautiful cupid is a beautiful love or some such, and as much as they might deny it they think a cupid with a hunched back or a gimp leg is some sort of sign of malformed love. Frankly though, once you've seen them laid and splayed on the autopsy slab, they're none of them that beautiful a sight and "malformation" is just a matter of metabiology. It doesn't mean shit. But this one was strange in a different way, all out of balance, this part too large for that, that part too small for this, some of the limbs and digits more fitted to a doll than a cupid. I don't remember who it was suggested we had a kiddy-fiddler, but as soon as the suggestion came up it seemed the obvious answer.

Here's the thing though. Forensics pulls all sorts of shit out of their ass, gives us a mugshot and a name, Frank Henderson, even points us at the right neighborhood. So we do some checking, and we haul this creep in, and he cops to it straight off. It was his cupid, sure enough, his and his niece's, and he'd killed it because he knew it was a fucking freak, that *he* was a fucking freak, that he was *enough* of a fucking freak, even, to twist a young girl's affection for her uncle into something that could spawn this…thing. I don't know that I believe his claim that he never touched her, even if we did lean on him hard enough to raise brutality charges in this more enlightened day and age. I don't know that I really care whether he's a sick fuck that acted on it or a sick fuck that didn't; either way he's a sick fuck. What gets in my head is the death of that love, cause I sure as hell don't think it's a fucking miracle of the human heart. Fuck, what gets in my head is I'm not even sure that cupid *was* a love; or if it was, what the fuck does that tell you about love? Some of the boys in the squad, they said it wasn't; that sort of shit just doesn't fucking qualify. But that just leaves me thinking, I've seen some pretty fucked-up loves in my time in Erocide. What else doesn't qualify? Cause I've damn sure seen some shit that walks the line.

Dumb or greedy. Blind or selfish. Or just plain crazy. People kill their love because that's what they are, Jackman used to say. But I wonder if it's maybe even more fucked up. Maybe that's what *they are* because that's what *their love is.*

Fuck, I don't know.

As a rookie, on the Armitage case, I thought I had it all figured out though. Love is desire that just keeps growing, right, becoming more and more solid by the day? It's wanting something, and wanting it even more after you've got it. So if someone's taken that away from you, most likely it's because of jealousy, because if they *can't* have it they don't see why you should. I had it all worked out.

I was right that it was jealousy, but wrong in every other way. When we brought the Armitages in to give their statements a day or so after the visit to the in-laws, the husband rolled immediately, gave himself up almost faster than we could get the fucking tape rolling. He told the whole story with a strange calm, like he'd locked all his feelings so deep inside he wasn't even connected to them anymore. It had been going wrong for a while, he said, since before they got married. He'd gotten moody and brooding when they weren't in company, barely spoke to her in the house; there were money problems and job worries he just couldn't open up to her about. She was diagnosed bipolar, so there were wild ups, but there were wild downs he couldn't deal with, times she said he didn't love her, just the idea of her. She knew he was kinda insecure, worried that he'd lose her to someone better-looking, more exciting. Fuck, it was a long and complicated story of two people letting their relationship fall apart for a huge sorry mess of reasons, of friendship and intimacy gradually crumbling into silence and distance. And yet their love didn't fade, both of them as sure as ever that they loved each other. It just seemed that, no matter how they felt, they couldn't *be* together. It didn't work. So he'd decided that he had to finish it.

She confirmed his story, eventually. They'd gone to the cinema and come back. She'd gone to bed and listened to him smashing glasses in the kitchen. Then something else shattered and she didn't just hear it; she felt it, in the atmosphere of the apartment and in her own heart. She got up, walked through to the kitchen, found him standing over the corpse of their love, the bloody baseball bat in his hand. And that was that.

He'd taken care of the body, and they'd sat up most of the night talking about what exactly they'd lost, what they were going to do now. She'd been ready to lie for him just to try and get them both through this sorry-ass shit-fest. Hell, they both *did* lie, when they called in the missing person's report, and when Jackman and me showed up to notify them that we'd found the body. They kept up the whole charade for two days, and I'm still not entirely sure why he caved so suddenly, changed his mind just like that. I remember him shrugging when I asked though.

I don't know, he said. *I don't know if I was sane then and I'm crazy now, or if I was crazy then and I'm sane now. I don't know anything anymore.*

So, yeah, you talk to Homicide, Narcotics, Vice, they'll all tell you that they've got the worst of it—the PTSD, and the alcohol abuse, and the relationship problems; but they ain't got nothing on Erocide. You look into the eyes of someone who's murdered their own love, I tell them, and there's a whole level of mindfuck you can't even imagine. A few bad dreams and a bit of a drink problem is chickenshit. But, fuck, show me a cop on Erocide who's even *got* a fucking relationship and I'll show you the next in line to put his weapon in his mouth and pull the trigger, blow his fucking brains out. The death of a love is a hard thing to take, but the worst thing is when you learn how to deal with it. Because the only way to deal with it is not to fucking love at all.

Fuck.

You walk long enough through the death of love, after a while you get to thinking…maybe those loves should never have lived at all.

Acknowledgements

On August 1st, 2008, I received an unexpected email from Bill Schafer, president of Subterranean Press, asking me if I'd be interested in compiling and editing a small fantasy anthology for them. I agreed, of course, but on the condition that a portion of the proceeds would go to breast cancer research. My mother had battled through breast cancer the year before, and it was important to me to give something back.

A lot of people have asked me since then why the hell Bill Schafer would give this opportunity to a green rookie like me. And to this day, I can't for the life of me tell you why. I suspect liquor may have had something to do with the decision. Who knows? Still, I'm grateful that he gave me this chance to experience the entire behind-the-scenes process firsthand. Hopefully he's as pleased with the results as I am.

I would like to thank my agent Matt Bialer for thinking that this was a great idea and letting me run along with it.

Special thanks go out to Yanni Kuznia and the rest of the SubPress crew for working hard to make the book you are holding in your hands a reality, and for putting up with all my questions and suggestions.

Many thanks to the authors who accepted the invitation to support this worthy cause. Hal Duncan, L. E. Modesitt, Jr., Celia S. Friedman, Tobias S. Buckell, and Brian Ruckley were a delight to work with from beginning to end. Sure, some will tell you that my editorial input was apropos and brought the best out of their short stories, but that's bullshit! Having such a talented lineup of authors certainly made my life a lot easier.

I would be remiss if I didn't extend my gratitude to those SFF writers who had to decline my invitation due to prior commitments and various other professional reasons. So thanks to Robin Hobb, Jacqueline Carey, Patrick Rothfuss, Richard Morgan, Stephen R. Donaldson, R. Scott Bakker, Guy Gavriel Kay, Joe Abercrombie, and all the others who offered kind words of encouragement.

I also owe a debt of gratitude to James Long, who graciously permitted me to use the name of his SFF book-reviewing blog, *Speculative Horizons*, for the title of this anthology. Check him out at www.speculativehorizons.blogspot.com.

Special thanks to Émilie Renaud for the gorgeous interior illustration. I fell in love with that art print the moment I laid eyes on it, and I knew I wanted it to be part of the anthology. But man did this girl make me work hard to finally convince her to agree to let me have it. Normally, I would hold that against her. There's only so much a guy can take, after all. Yet for introducing me to the body of work of the genius Hayao Miyazaki, I'll be eternally grateful to her. Don't you hate when that happens!?!

Last but not least, I want to thank everyone who has made Pat's Fantasy Hotlist one of the most popular speculative fiction blogs out there. I'm not deluding myself. I'm aware that I was granted this opportunity because I have a vast and loyal audience. Exactly why so many of you keep returning in droves to read the drivel I post on an almost daily basis, I'll never know. I'm not sure how long I'll keep reviewing SFF material, but you guys certainly made this adventure one hell of a ride for me. "Wasting technology since January 2005" is our motto, so here's to hoping that we still have a few good times ahead of us!

Compiling and editing *Speculative Horizons* was a fascinating learning experience for me. In the end, this anthology turned out even better than I ever thought it would. Which is why I'm proud to finally share it with you.

All the best,

Patrick St-Denis
October 27th, 2009